FORSAKING ALL OTHERS

Dr Shirley Baxter, after several inexcusable mistakes, leaves her London hospital to look after her sick grandfather in Inverdorran. However, with the help of locum Dr Andrews, he soon recovers. Shirley meets and falls in love with Neil Fraser who is working hard to build a local leisure centre. But Neil's plans are beset with problems and, after he suffers a breakdown, Shirley finds her medical training is once again in demand.

Books by Jane Carrick
in the Linford Romance Library:

DIAMONDS ON THE LAKE
A PEARL FOR LOVE
A HANDFUL OF MIST
THE COURAGE OF ANNA CAMERON
FACE OF A STRANGER
MY DARLING GERALDINE
GERALDINE'S WAR
LOVE MUST BE SURE
SO GOLDEN THEIR HARVEST

JANE CARRICK

FORSAKING ALL OTHERS

Complete and Unabridged

LINFORD
Leicester

First published in Great Britain in 1977

First Linford Edition
published 2006

British Library CIP Data

Carrick, Jane
Forsaking all others.—Large print ed.—
Linford romance library
1. Love stories
2. Large type books
I. Title
823.9′14 [F]

ISBN 1–84617–143–1

Published by
F. A. Thorpe (Publishing)
Anstey, Leicestershire

Set by Words & Graphics Ltd.
Anstey, Leicestershire
Printed and bound in Great Britain by
T. J. International Ltd., Padstow, Cornwall

This book is printed on acid-free paper

Like A Miracle

Dr Shirley Baxter stared out of the staff room window at the well-kept lawns and neat flower-beds of the large teaching hospital which had become so familiar to her over the past few months.

It was a view which had never failed to excite her, ever since she had arrived in London from her home in New Zealand, but now she was seeing it through a mist of tears.

Shirley thought of the years she had spent training in New Zealand, and of the absorbing work she had done on virus diseases, so that when she got the chance to study new techniques in this large teaching hospital, she had grabbed it eagerly.

The hospital had been short-staffed and she had been thrown in at the deep end, but she had welcomed the responsibility and had been caught up in the devotion and dedication which her work demanded.

The first mistake she had made had shocked her deeply, and she would never forget the fact that if it had not been for Sister Leila Reynolds, the consequences could have been serious.

Shirley had gone off duty realising just how tired she was. During the past few days there had been a build-up of very urgent cases and she had not noticed her own fatigue in helping to deal with the work involved. Even so, she had only managed to sleep that night after taking a sleeping tablet.

Looking back, Shirley could see that her confidence had been shaken from then on. It was Brian Wills, a fellow doctor, who had picked up a chart she had filled in and laughed gently when she had confused two lots of information.

But although it made amusing reading, Shirley had not even smiled. It was another mistake and she could not afford mistakes in her job.

Then a week later, Shirley had been about to put a dressing on a patient without checking for allergy. Although a quick-thinking staff nurse had drawn her aside with a diplomatic query before any harm had been done, she had felt she had reached the end of the road.

Somehow or other she'd got her lines crossed. She had thought herself to be a born doctor, following in the footsteps of her Scottish grandfather, but it was obvious to her that she just wasn't capable of the constant vigilance needed in her work.

Even Sister Reynolds had shown concern when Shirley inadvertently dropped a hint that she might be giving up medicine. But it was her own decision, and now she had handed in her resignation to the Chief.

'He was so nice about it,' she said to Brian, forcing back the tears and taking a sip of scalding hot coffee, 'but I think he recognises that — that I'm not much use to him now.'

'More likely he recognises that you'll come running back if he lets you go now,' Brian said. 'What are you planning to do in the future?'

'Oh, get a job where my theoretic knowledge might prove useful without any patients to kill off. Though I had rather promised to go and see my grandfather in Scotland first of all. I'm not really looking forward to telling him. We've never met, you see.'

'Oh, yes. I think you mentioned he was a doctor.'

'Still practising, though he's seventy-five. Or rather, keeping his hand in. He lives in a place called Inverdorran.'

Brian's 'bleeper' sounded and he put down his coffee mug.

'Duty calls,' he said. 'I'll see you later, my dear. Don't forget, I'll need your Inverdorran address!'

Shirley nodded, then gathered herself together to go to her own duties in the lab, having been excused the wards at her own request. She should be feeling

4

an enormous sense of relief, but somehow it wasn't there. Instead, she felt as though something had died in her.

She thought about her grandfather and the fact that she was due to go and visit him the following weekend, and of his disappointment when he learned about the failure of her career.

Sitting down, she hastily penned him a letter, excusing herself for another week or two. Somehow she felt she would have to be in command of herself a great deal more before meeting Dr Hamish Baxter for the first time. She wanted a new job and a settled future.

* * *

Over the next two weeks, Shirley began to pull herself together, and even enjoyed giving lectures to the new intake, as a change from her lab work. When she was called to the telephone one afternoon, she walked briskly, expecting to hear from one of the friends she had made in London.

But it was a rather crackly line, and a woman's voice with the soft, Scottish lilt she had loved to hear in her father.

'Dr Baxter? This is Mrs Ross. I'm housekeeper to your grandfather.'

'Oh . . . Oh yes . . . Mrs Ross . . . '

'Dr Baxter has taken ill — pneumonia — the doctor says his condition is critical. I . . . I thought you'd better be told, Miss Baxter . . . er . . . Dr Baxter . . . '

'I'll be with you as soon as I can, Mrs Ross,' she said decisively.

'Oh, thank you, Miss Shirley . . . '

In her relief, Mrs Ross called her by her christian name and Shirley felt oddly comforted, yet left with a great sense of urgency.

Suddenly her mind was working more clearly than it had done for some time, as she again asked to see the Chief Medical Officer and was excused from working out the last of her notice.

The train service was not very

satisfactory, she thought, studying a timetable with Sister Reynolds, who was proving a good friend.

'You could hire a car, but it would be a marathon drive,' Leila Reynolds said doubtfully.

'Oh, I don't mind driving,' Shirley said. 'I used to drive for miles back home. The roads will be quiet if I drive overnight, and I — I feel that every second counts.'

'You see to the car and pack a case. I'll get you some road maps and a flask or two of coffee and sandwiches.'

'Oh, bless you,' Shirley said, then hesitated, writing down her grand-father's address.

Brian was on duty and could not be disturbed, so she gave the address to Sister Reynolds.

'Could you please tell Dr Wills I had to rush away? I'm sorry I can't stay to say goodbye.'

Leila Reynolds' fine dark eyes shad-owed a little, but her warm smile was quick.

'Of course, Dr Baxter,' she said. 'I'll explain it all to Dr Wills.'

★ ★ ★

Later, Shirley could not remember very much about the journey north to Inverdorran. She'd had to get used to the car, but soon it was responding well, and she drove it to the limit up the motorway, stopping only twice for a break.

What would her grandfather be like, she wondered. Was she too late in making this visit?

Somehow, she had always pictured him as an older version of her father, knowing that he had often said he and his father were too much alike. It had led to rows and quarrels as Colin was growing up, when his father could not understand why he should ever want to leave the country where he had been born, even though Colin had itchy feet and longed to see a bit of the world.

After one quarrel, which seemed to

bring everything to a head, he had walked out and started hitching his way round the world, working at any and every job which came his way.

He eventually arrived in New Zealand and got a job sheep shearing. There he had met Kate Wilson, a lovely girl of Scots background, and had settled down at last.

Shirley was born the following year. Her brother, Paul, who was nineteen, and sixteen-year-old Nancy were still in New Zealand.

Ten years ago, Colin Baxter had returned to Scotland when his mother died, and Shirley remembered how much she had wanted to go with him but for the fact that she was sitting important examinations at the time.

When Shirley showed signs of wanting to study medicine, Colin Baxter had eyed her thoughtfully.

'You can never go against what has been born in you,' he told her, 'as I know. Your mother and I will help you all we can. Your grandfather will be very pleased and proud.'

Soon she was writing regularly to her grandfather in Inverdorran. Somehow he had been with her, all the way through her career, and now he was very sick.

She had been driving steadily for some time before she noticed with horror that steam was rising from beneath the bonnet of the car. She put her foot on the brake and the car slowed down gradually, eventually stopping inconveniently on a bend, but Shirley was too tired to care.

Shirley opened the bonnet of the car gingerly to let most of the steam escape and gazed despairingly under it.

The air on the open hillside was becoming cool as the sky clouded overhead and, rather than catch a chill, Shirley returned despondently to the comparative warmth of the inside of the car.

She had not been there long, when in her mirror she saw a Land-Rover approaching at some speed. With a flash of annoyance, she noted that the driver was obviously a man seething with impatience, as he began to flash his lights and hoot his horn.

There was nothing she could do for there was absolutely no way of allowing him to pass.

The driver eventually pulled up within inches of her back bumper and leapt out of the car, to stride purposefully towards her.

In spite of her predicament, Shirley could not help noticing that he was very lithe and good looking, his skin well tanned and his dark hair curling neatly about his head.

'What a stupid place to park a car! Have you absolutely no sense?' he demanded angrily.

Shirley felt faint with dismay and by now was feeling the weight of weariness pressing upon her.

'I'm sorry, Mr . . . '

'Neil Fraser.' He paused. 'Where are you heading for?'

'Inverdorran.'

'Hmm.' Neil Fraser looked at her thoughtfully, seeing the signs of fatigue on her face. She didn't look a stupid girl, so it must have been tiredness which made her stop in such a foolish place.

He bit his lip, looking at his watch to see if he would have time to take her all the way to the village. Yet he had some parcels to deliver to the station to meet the two o'clock train from Edinburgh.

'There's a garage farther along the road where it forks to Inverdorran and Aviemore,' he said. 'I'm going to Aviemore, so I shall drop you there. You can arrange to have your car fixed.'

'Thank you,' she said in a subdued voice.

★ ★ ★

It was a one-man garage, and the owner did not seem disposed towards being very helpful. He looked at Shirley rather stolidly as she did her best to explain the situation.

'I have no car for hire and no taxi,' he told her, shaking his head. 'I'll pick up your car for you, but I haven't another to hire out.'

Shirley pushed a hand through her dark chestnut hair and thought that this must surely be the last straw! To be so near, yet held up in the last mile or two! She looked at the name . . . *Fairway Garage, Jock Sinclair, proprietor.*

She was aware of a woman coming from the direction of the house attached to the garage, no doubt Mrs Sinclair.

'Is there anywhere I could wash?' she asked. 'And telephone?'

Perhaps Mrs Ross could do something for her.

'My grandfather is very ill in Inverdorran, and Mrs Ross is expecting me.'

'Your grandfather?' asked the woman. 'Would that be . . . ?'

'Dr Hamish Baxter.'

'Och, now why didn't you say so before?' the man said. 'If it hadn't been for the doctor, I wouldn't have Janet, here, beside me today. So you're the doctor's granddaughter. Well, well! I'm Jock Sinclair and this is my wife, Janet.'

'And you'd better get the pick-up wagon out,' Janet Sinclair said with mock severity, then turned quickly to Shirley. 'There's a wee cup of tea in the pot. Take a sip at a cup, even though you are in a hurry, Miss Baxter. Jock will have the wagon ready in no time.'

The tea was refreshing but Shirley didn't take time to finish the cup. Her sense of urgency was now very great, though she listened while Mr Sinclair kept up a long eulogy to her grandfather all the way to Inverdorran, pulling up outside Beech House, the big old-fashioned house where her grandfather had lived all his life, and where her father had been born.

* * *

'Never fear about your car. I'll arrange everything,' Mr Sinclair told her cheerfully. 'Och, we've all been worried about the doctor, but he'll be fine now you've come to help . . . '

He was out of the pick-up and ringing the bell, when suddenly a motherly woman of about fifty opened the door.

'I've brought your young lady,' Mr Sinclair said, and Shirley hardly had time to thank the garage owner before she was ushered into the big comfortable lounge, full of chintz-covered chairs, and with a cheery fire burning in the grate.

A pleasant-looking man in his twenties got up to greet her.

'This is Dr Andrews,' Mrs Ross said, leading Shirley into the room. 'You must be very tired, my dear.'

Shirley nodded, but her whole concern was for her grandfather.

'How is he, Dr Andrews?' she asked anxiously. 'I've been worried all the way north.'

'He's holding his own, Miss Baxter. I wouldn't like to say more than that at the moment. I'm just going up. Do you want to come with me now, or have a rest first?'

'I'll come now,' Shirley said quickly. She would rest much easier after she had seen the old man for herself.

★ ★ ★

It felt strangely unreal to be walking up the broad stairs to the large bedroom overlooking the front of the house. Everything in the house seemed to be large and comfortable and had seen a great many years of constant use.

The bedroom was full of heavy, old-fashioned furniture and there was the faint sweet smell of lavender mingling with antiseptic.

Shirley's eyes were all for the still figure lying on the bed and it seemed, in her tired state, that she had become two people, the doctor and the granddaughter.

He was her own flesh and blood, she thought, her eyes devouring the strong features and leonine head covered with

16

thick white hair.

'He's holding his own for a man of his age,' said Dr Andrews, 'though Dr Baxter has always been a strong man, out in all weathers. His strong constitution is standing him in good stead, otherwise . . . ' His gaze was meaningful, and Shirley nodded.

She found herself desperately wanting her grandfather to live, the strange feeling coming over her that they had need of one another. How much she wanted to know him, and be with him in the years to come!

Dr Andrews was still talking as he led the way back downstairs.

'By the way, Mrs Ross says you're a fully-fledged doctor yourself, so we have two Dr Baxters, as it were. I can't tell you how glad I am about that. I have my own practice, you know, and I'm helping out here as best I can, but I couldn't half do with an extra pair of hands . . . ' He saw the girl turn very white, her eyes dark ringed.

'I'm — I'm sorry, Dr Andrews, but I

shan't be able to help,' she told him. 'I — I won't be practising medicine . . . '

'Not practising!'

'I'm sorry,' she repeated.

'Oh — well I'm sorry, too, Miss Baxter,' he said quietly. 'I've misunderstood, obviously. Oh well, I'll be back, of course. I've no doubt you and Mrs Ross between you will make excellent nurses, though.'

'I'll — we'll do our best,' Shirley promised.

In the big kitchen, Mrs Ross prepared bacon and eggs when she found out that Shirley had had nothing to eat for some time, and the girl sat on an ancient rocking chair with carved wooden swan heads and necks for arms, and a black horse-hair seat.

She was desperately tired.

'I'll take you round the house and garden,' Mrs Ross was promising. 'I've known it all my life. I've always lived around here.'

'Those roses look beautiful,' Shirley said, staring out at the garden.

'The very best,' said Mrs Ross. 'The doctor's an expert, though he claims he's only an amateur rose breeder. But just come outside here, Miss Shirley . . . I mean Dr Baxter . . . '

'Miss Shirley will do.' Shirley smiled, though her eyes went rather bleak.

'Well, see here then, Miss Shirley.' Mrs Ross led the way into a large greenhouse. 'Just look at all these seedlings coming up. The doctor has been hybridising for forty years and his best stock is all out here in this large walled plot. He keeps the gate locked, and only he attends to it.

'I — I think it was great company, especially after Colin — your father — went away. Many a one comes to talk roses with him, as well as medicine. One of his friends is doing his best to produce a blue rose, but the doctor is trying for a pure white one which has still retained its wonderful perfume.

'So many roses have had their perfume sacrificed to beauty, or so he says, but he thinks the perfume is just as important. He's near his white rose now, Miss Shirley. This new crop could contain the Shirley Baxter . . . '

'Shirley Baxter!'

'After his wife, my dear, though, of course, it will be you, too, won't it? That's why I feel that the doctor will pull through. He's determined to grow that perfect white rose.'

'I'm sure he will,' Shirley said, her ears feeling muffled.

Suddenly Mrs Ross was aware of her fatigue, and was chiding herself for not having noticed before.

'You can borrow one of my night-dresses,' she said, 'till you get your case.'

It was bright pink and much too large for Shirley, but she didn't care. Soon she was between lavender-scented sheets in a bed which felt as though it had been made out of feathers. Before her head touched the pillow, Shirley was asleep.

Her last mental vision was one of Neil Fraser as he walked towards her from his Land-Rover. She felt she would never forget her first impression of him.

★   ★   ★

It seemed many hours later that Shirley woke again to the sound of voices, one of them a man's. It had been the deepest and most refreshing sleep she'd had in months, and for a moment she lay still, luxuriating in the warmth and comfort of her large bed.

She leapt out of bed and, after a quick bath, during which she could hear conversation and even the faint sounds of a woman singing downstairs, she dressed in her plain suit, combed her lovely dark chestnut hair and ran lightly downstairs.

If it was Dr Andrews, she wanted to have a word with him.

But it was a young man around Neil Fraser's age who leapt to his feet as she entered the sitting-room, his mouth almost falling open at the sight of her.

Mrs Ross's eyes twinkled as she reflected that for once he had been effectively silenced.

'This is Mr Geoffrey Lewis, our schoolteacher,' she introduced. 'Dr Shirley Baxter.' They shook hands.

'Mr Lewis has brought your car back,' Mrs Ross said by way of explanation.

'Oh!' Shirley cried. 'Oh, I see. That's great. Thank you very much. I can get my luggage out of the boot now.'

'Oh, no, you must allow me,' Geoffrey Lewis said eagerly. 'I — I lodge with Mr and Mrs Sinclair, you know. I was only too happy to bring the car back.'

Shirley smiled, eyeing him curiously. His accent was unfamiliar to her.

'You aren't from these parts then, Mr Lewis?'

'Oh, Geoff will do — if that's all right. I mean, I get enough of Mr Lewis at school. No, I'm a Geordie. Tyneside, you know,' he explained when she still looked puzzled.

'Oh, yes. Near Newcastle.'

'Gateshead actually, though I've been teaching in Inverdorran since I qualified. It's a great place. I — I've just been trying to make Mrs Ross remember some old poems and songs . . . '

'Och, he's always at everybody with his tape recorder.' Mrs Ross laughed. 'Making them sing or remember wee poems or children's rhymes even. He fair . . . '

'Bores everybody into the ground,' Geoff said ruefully. 'I know. But it's criminal the way you all neglect your own heritage. Do you know, Miss Baxter . . . '

'Dr Baxter,' put in Mrs Ross.

'If I could have the keys of my car, and the bill,' Shirley said gently, and Geoffrey Lewis coloured again. He was an enthusiast, and she had no wish to be caught up in his enthusiasms at the moment.

'Of course,' he said, fishing in his pocket. 'There's no charge, though. Jock Sinclair says he still owes a lot more to your grandfather.'

'Oh, but . . . '

'No, he would be offended. But I can see you'll have a lot to do, Miss . . . er . . . Doctor. I'll just get your cases and carry them up.'

He didn't look strong enough, Shirley thought, yet his arms were sinewy as he carried her luggage up to her bedroom, then blushed as he said he hoped to see her again some time.

'Oh dear, Mr Lewis is a very energetic young man,' Mrs Ross said, closing the door. 'But very well thought of, Miss Shirley, especially by the ones who want to keep Inverdorran as it is, without it getting spoilt.'

'Spoilt? Who would ever want to spoil Inverdorran?' Shirley asked.

'You'd be surprised,' Mrs Ross said darkly. 'It's the new road, of course.'

'New road?'

'Yes, a fine new road from the South, and a fine bridge to be built. Och, we'll get plenty of tourists then.'

Shirley had been remembering her

nightmare journey along the road, and had been mentally applauding the making of a new road. But now the aspect of big changes being brought, and an influx of tourists, made her pause for thought.

'Mr Lewis was able to put into words what a lot of people felt, that the people coming in their crowds like that would destroy the very beauty they had come to see. Your grandfather felt it could not have been put better.'

'I can see what he means,' Shirley said, looking out on a magnificent view of distant mountains and the faint silvery streak of water beyond.

'Of course there are others all up in arms against Mr Lewis since they would be making a bit of money for themselves, with bed and breakfast, and so on. The Fraser boys would do best out of it. They are busy building a fine big sports complex with pitch and putt, tennis, sailing, canoeing. Oh . . . and pony-trekking. They are going to provide everything they can think of.'

'The Fraser boys?' Shirley asked, then remembered it was a common name round here, and the young man she had met had been going to Aviemore.

'Of course, they've worked for it,' Mrs Ross went on, 'on the oil rigs, you know. Neil spent years on the rigs, where they earn a lot of money, and he's saved every penny.

'Now he's bought sailing dinghies and ponies and he's putting his back into making this great sports place, so you can imagine that he and Mr Lewis don't get on.' She paused and frowned.

'Mind you, I think he has worked twice as hard since Catriona jilted him. He's all the businessman now.'

★ ★ ★

The following morning, Shirley went into the bedroom to see her grandfather before Dr Andrews' visit, finding him very restless, his forehead wet with perspiration.

She sponged him carefully, talking to him in a soothing tone, while she and Mrs Ross made up his bed, and eventually he fell asleep.

Shirley watched him for a while, her hand on his pulse.

'His breathing seems easier,' she said to the older woman, who nodded.

'I think so, too, Dr Shirley,' she said, watching the girl's deft movements, and thinking that there were, indeed, two doctors in the house!

After breakfast, Shirley looked out at the bright sunshine. She had not, as yet, explored Inverdorran and there were many places her father had urged her to visit, places such as the old ruined keep on the hillside, the stepping stones at a shallow bend in the river, and an old mill with an ancient water wheel.

It was quiet and peaceful in the rambling village, but as she neared home, she could hear the children playing in the park and paused for a moment near the railings to watch them at play.

Shirley slowly turned towards Beech House again, when suddenly there was a scream, and she saw a small boy lying on the concrete, having fallen off a swing. He was already picking himself up as she rushed towards him, his small face white, his leg spouting blood from a nasty cut. A little girl, obviously his younger sister, looked on fearfully, her eyes filling with tears when she saw the cut.

'Jamie's leg is broken,' she whispered.

'Of course it isn't,' Shirley said briskly. 'I'm a doctor, and I should know. Come on, the pair of you, up to the surgery, and I'll fix it for him.'

She bent down, doing some quick first-aid with her handkerchief, then hurried the children towards Beech House.

Mrs Ross saw them from the window and ran to open the door.

'I don't suppose Dr Andrews is here yet?' Shirley asked.

'Not yet, Dr Shirley. Och, poor wee Jamie, he's got a nasty cut there . . . '

'Could I have the key to the medicine cupboard then, please, Mrs Ross? I'll have to attend to this myself.

Mrs Ross handed over a bunch of keys and the second one opened the cupboard in the surgery.

Shirley undid her makeshift bandage, and cleaned the wound properly. It was a deep cut, and wasn't too easily dealt with since it required a stitch. He was a game little boy, she thought, looking at his pale face and frightened eyes, but he was determined not to cry.

Mrs Ross had appeared with mugs of cocoa.

'I thought this would warm them up,' she said. 'Wee Fiona's had as big a fright as Jamie.'

'Where do they live? I'd better get the car out,' Shirley said.

'At the Frasers' farm, just on the outskirts.'

'I can show you,' Fiona offered shyly, and Shirley ruffled her hair.

'Good girl,' she said.

It wasn't far out of the village to the

tidy-looking farm on the hillside. A young woman, pausing to look at the car as she crossed the farmyard, ran to them in alarm as Shirley helped Jamie from the car.

'I'm afraid Jamie has cut his leg rather badly,' Shirley told her. 'I'm Dr Baxter's granddaughter, and I've done all I can for him at the moment, but if it shows no sign of healing in a day or so, then I think you ought to consult Dr Andrews.'

'Oh! Oh dear . . . I can't thank you enough, Miss . . . Miss Baxter. Oh dear, Jamie, what have you been up to?'

'We had cocoa,' Fiona said proudly.

Shirley laughed and left the children to tell their tale. She felt oddly elated that she had managed to cope so quickly and so easily with Jamie's injured leg. Yet anyone with the smallest skill in first-aid would have done the same.

Rushing to cope with an emergency was a different thing from a full-time practice. Cases of long-term illness weren't quite the same as dealing with an accident to a child.

★   ★   ★

She garaged the car, then stuck her hands in her pockets as she walked round to the back of the house, her fingers closing on the bunch of keys. Amongst them was the big old-fashioned key to the locked rose garden. On impulse, Shirley paused, then walked back to the gate, opening the heavy lock, and slipping in to look at the rose bushes which had been her grandfather's delight for so many years.

Should she water them in a dry spell, she wondered. Was there anyone who could advise her? They all looked healthy enough and well cared for at the moment, but she would hate anything to happen to the bushes because of neglect.

Shirley made a mental note to get some advice, and as she turned away, her eyes fell on the opened bud on one of the new plants which Mrs Ross had pointed out to her.

Bending forward, she stared at the most exquisite white rose she had ever seen. On impulse, she fished in her bag for a small knife and snipped off the bloom, sniffing its glorious perfume, then going into the house to find a narrow weighted glass to hold the rose.

Carrying it up to the bedside table beside her grandfather's bed, she looked down on his sleeping face, then as she was about to turn away, his eyes suddenly opened.

For a long moment they gazed at one another, then her grandfather's eyes seemed to light up in wonder.

'Shirley!' he whispered. 'My lovely . . . Shirley . . . ' His eyes closed again, and this time there was no doubt that his breathing was easier.

A moment later, Shirley heard the gate creaking and saw that a car had drawn up outside. It would be Dr Andrews, she decided, hurrying downstairs before he could ring the bell.

But as she threw open the door, she found herself staring up into the thin, dark face of Neil Fraser.

Shirley's heart lurched at the sight of him, and he looked rather taken aback to see her.

'Oh — so it's you,' he said awkwardly. 'I called to — to thank you on Ellen's behalf. She sent these eggs to thank you for bandaging Jamie's leg. We're very grateful. He isn't the strongest of boys.'

'I'm glad I happened to be there. You've got a brave little son, Mr Fraser.'

'Oh, Jamie isn't my son. He's my brother David's boy. I'm the bachelor in the family.'

He grinned a little, though she thought she saw a flash of pain in his eyes, and remembered Mrs Ross saying something about a girl called Catriona.

'Do come in,' Shirley said, leading the way into the sitting-room from the hall.

'I really came to ask after the doctor,'

Neil said. 'I think the whole village is anxious.'

'I'm beginning to feel a little more hopeful about him,' Shirley said. 'I've a feeling he is on the mend. Do come and have a look at him.'

Softly, they tiptoed into the bedroom, and Shirley paused, almost with shock, when she saw that her grandfather was fully awake.

'Hello, Neil, so it's you,' he said, his voice a great deal stronger. 'I see you've met my granddaughter. I knew she would come. I knew she would take over from me till I get on my feet again.'

Shirley stared at the old man, stunned. It was almost like a miracle the way her grandfather had recovered, but how could she tell him now that she had no intention of ever practising medicine again?

Seeking Advice

Shirley hurried forward to the bed, taking her grandfather's hand in her own, a hint of tears in her eyes. Beside her, Neil Fraser was expressing his surprise at Dr Baxter's words, not knowing that they were the first he had spoken for some time.

'I should have guessed that Miss Baxter was a doctor. She's just attended to my nephew after he hurt his leg. That's Jamie, you know — David's son . . . '

His voice tailed off as he saw that the old man and young girl were gazing at one another, as though unaware of anyone else in the world. The old man was smiling as she took his hand and they took stock of one another.

'You're a good lass,' he whispered, his voice weakening again. 'I'll tell Colin when — when I see him . . . ' But now the old man's eyes were closing again, his breathing easing. He seemed to be completely relaxed now he knew she was close beside him.

'We'll leave him to sleep,' she said softly.

'Yes, I must be getting home. I've got a lot to attend to.'

'Thank you for the eggs,' Shirley said, opening the door, and was startled to see young Dr Andrews almost on the doorstep. He didn't look as neat and tidy as he usually did and even Neil Fraser could see he was completely worn out.

'Sorry I'm late,' he greeted Shirley, 'but I've had to put in rather a lot of calls for my own practice.'

'Well, Miss Baxter here — or I should say *Dr* Baxter — should be able to help you,' Neil said.

'Only she isn't practising at the moment,' Dr Andrews said briefly, so that Shirley flushed uncomfortably as she turned to bid goodbye to Neil Fraser. She saw the puzzled look on his face, then he seemed to shrug a little as he walked away.

Shirley sighed as she led Dr Andrews into the sitting-room.

'Let me get you a cup of tea before you do any more. Grandfather is sleeping at the moment, and he's been much better,' she said. 'I — I'm sorry you're having such a lot of work to do. You look fit to drop.'

Dr Andrews looked at her, his eyes weary. He was a solid, dependable-looking man, but now he bore that special look which she had seen often among doctors in hospital wards after a rush of illness or accident. He had more than he could cope with.

'I'd welcome a cup of tea,' he told her, and lowered himself on to the settee.

She hurried into the kitchen, where she put on the electric kettle and began to cut some ham sandwiches, though her thoughts were still with Dr Andrews.

Shirley's hand shook violently even as

she picked up the teapot. She breathed deeply to calm herself before hurrying through to the sitting-room.

The young doctor had fallen asleep, his tumbled hair damp on his forehead so that it seemed criminal to wake him, but as she put the tray down on a small table, his bright blue eyes opened and he stared at her.

'Oh, sorry. I — I fell asleep.'

'Don't apologise.' Quietly she poured the tea, though again her heart was beating loud enough for her to hear. She had to do something to help.

'Look, Dr Andrews. I — I feel I would like to help a little, if I can. I don't like to see you with — with so much work that you can't cope . . . '

The young doctor looked at the girl's shadowed face, feeling there was something behind her attitude he didn't quite understand. Shirley Baxter's decision not to practise medicine was no light one.

'I could certainly do with you taking evening surgery for me on Thursday,' he said slowly. 'I'm supposed to be at a conference in Inverness then, and I had been wondering how to divide myself in two.'

Shirley nodded gravely. She was beginning to like Dr Andrews, and found something comforting and dependable about him.

'You wouldn't find it too strenuous, I'm sure,' he told her.

'Then of course I'll be delighted to help,' she assured him, fighting down any misgivings. 'Can I pour you more tea?'

'No, thanks. That was wonderful.' He smiled gratefully. 'Now I'd better see your grandfather and be on my way.'

* * *

That night Shirley slept better than she expected, and ran downstairs much refreshed in the morning, after her usual visit to her grandfather.

Once more the old man had woken for a brief spell, and asked about various things which were on his mind, and about patients whom he had been attending.

'The Dewar baby has arrived and it's a boy,' Shirley told him, 'and old Mrs Clark has got her daughter staying now, so she'll be looked after.'

'Are you settling in, lass?' Hamish Baxter whispered. 'Have you got all you need?'

'Yes, Grandfather, I'm fine.'

'Use my car. Charge up the petrol and I'll sign a cheque. There's no need to worry about household matters. Mrs Ross is very competent.'

Again he fell asleep, and Shirley went on downstairs thoughtfully. She would use her grandfather's old car, but she would also have to return the hired one to London, and settle the account, since it looked as though she would have to stay here in Inverdorran for a week or two yet. The days were beginning to be eaten up with commitments.

She was still pondering the problem

later in the morning after she had
walked along to change the bandage on
Jamie Fraser's leg, and almost ran into
Geoffrey Lewis, the young teacher who
had brought the hired car back from
Sinclair's garage.

'Hi there, Miss Baxter,' he called
cheerily, clutching an armful of books.
'Dr Baxter, I should say . . . '

'Oh — sorry,' she said, startled. Her
thoughts had been miles away. 'I didn't
notice you.'

'You were obviously working out all
your problems.' Geoffrey grinned. 'How
is your patient?'

'My patient? Oh, you mean Grandfather! Oh, he's pulling round. It will take
a while yet, but he's definitely on the
mend.'

'Then you're still staying on here?'
Geoffrey asked, falling into step beside
her.

'Well, for a little while at least.' She
had been so preoccupied she had
hardly remembered who he was at first.
The conversation turned to the hired

car which Geoffrey had brought home for her after it had been repaired.

'I shall have to return it,' she said. 'The sooner it goes back, the better.'

'You like Inverdorran then?' Geoffrey asked, his eyes ranging round to the far distant hills.

'It's beautiful,' she agreed, smiling.

'People come from quite a distance to look at all this lovely scenery,' he said, 'but some would spoil it for the sake of cashing in on it. They would spoil the very thing people come to see.'

'In what way?'

'By providing what they call amenities . . . a big new road, cafés, etc. It'll just look like anywhere else once all that gets shoved up.'

Shirley said nothing. She had not, as yet, given the subject much thought, and remembered that Mrs Ross had told her it was Neil Fraser who was all out to put up the 'amenities.'

'Don't you agree, Dr Baxter?' Geoffrey Lewis was asking earnestly. 'Don't you agree that we've got to unite to fight off these kinds of changes?'

'I've only just arrived here, Mr Lewis. I haven't heard the other side.'

'There shouldn't be another side — and Geoffrey will do.'

'Well — Geoffrey — I'd rather wait till I've been here a little while before expressing an opinion.'

'Aren't you interested in the history of the place?'

'Of course.'

'I'm going to Edinburgh on Thursday,' he went on eagerly, 'to the Historical Society. There's a weekend conference — wait a moment!' He paused, staring at her. 'I could take your car back for you. There's a branch of the car-hire firm there. I could help share the expense of it because it would suit me very well to drive down, and get the train back home.'

Shirley's eyes lit up. 'Oh, are you sure, Mr Lewis — I mean Geoffrey? Why, that would be wonderful, and would solve a problem for me.'

'Of course. I'll be glad to do it,' he assured her.

'I'll have all the information ready for you then, and if you'll just pay the car-hire people for me . . . '

'It will be a pleasure,' he told her heartily. 'We can square up when I get back home again.'

★ ★ ★

Shirley again smiled with relief as she parted from Geoffrey Lewis outside Beech House.

Mrs Ross greeted her warmly as she went into the kitchen, having seen the young man walking with her to the door. It was nice for a young lady to have a career, she thought, but nicer still to see her married and settled down with a nice young man.

And Miss Shirley did not seem to lack admirers!

'There's a telephone message on a pad in the hall,' she said. 'A Dr Wills.'

'Oh,' Shirley said, surprised and

pleased. It would be so nice to have a word with Brian again.

'Did he leave a number for me to ring back?'

'No, but he said he was going on duty and that he hopes to get a break soon and come to see you, here, in Inverdorran.'

'That will be lovely,' Shirley said. It was funny how nice things could happen, even when one's whole mind seemed to be full of worries.

For the next two days Shirley had cause to be anxious again about her grandfather. As he regained strength, he was inclined to lose it again, questioning her excitedly or worrying over trifling matters, then lying back, restless and feverish.

Shirley found herself trying to anticipate his worries, and again her thoughts went to his wonderful collection of roses.

'I wish I knew what to do about them,' she confessed to Mrs Ross as she sat down to a belated tea.

'Do about what?' the older woman asked, her eyes smiling. Shirley had her grandfather's habit of thinking aloud.

'Oh — the roses,' Shirley said, smiling self-consciously. 'They've been on my mind for a couple of days.'

'Oh dear, that reminds me. It's my turn to be forgetful,' Mrs Ross said. 'Brigadier Maxwell rang up yesterday.'

'Brigadier Maxwell?'

'Yes, though he's retired now from the Army. He and your grandfather are cronies, if you can put it like that, since they're always arguing over their roses.'

'He's another grower, then?'

'He is, though not as good as the doctor, mind. Maybe I should say they're rivals rather than cronies,' Mrs Ross said hurriedly. 'Nobody can grow roses like the doctor.

'Only, Brigadier Maxwell was asking about the doctor's bushes. Maybe it would be a good idea to talk to him. He didn't exactly offer his help, but you might get some advice out of him at least.'

Shirley's face lit up as she looked at her watch. She had promised her grandfather that she would sit with him for a little while, but he was dozing at the moment.

'Where does Brigadier Maxwell live?'

'In that big house, painted white, on the road out towards the Frasers' place. You've got to turn off, up a wee side road, and you'll see some ground being cleared to the left.

'That's the Frasers' ground where they're supposed to be building a big new restaurant or motel or something. But that's a bit farther along the road, so if you come to that, you've missed Ardlui. That's what the Maxwells call their house.'

'I see. Well, I'll call in and thank him for his phone call. I'd like to see how he really feels about helping with Grandfather's roses.'

Shirley found the charming old white-painted house quite easily, and rang the bell. After a second ring, a white-haired upright man appeared round the side of the house. He wore a green apron and was wiping his hands on a rough towel.

'Good afternoon . . . Brigadier Maxwell? I'm Shirley Baxter,' she said, walking forward. 'I believe you rang up the other day?'

The elderly man turned beetroot red and seemed to hesitate for a moment before coming forward.

'Oh — oh yes,' he said, putting out a hand to shake hers. She noticed that his bore one or two scratches. 'I spoke to Mrs Ross. So you're Dr Baxter's granddaughter. You'd better come in.'

* * *

Shirley followed him into the house almost reluctantly, not feeling at all sure whether she was really welcome or not. Somehow she did not think the Brigadier was going to be free and easy about giving her advice over the roses.

Yet a glance at one or two vases of

cut flowers, as she walked through the hall, hardened her resolution. Her grandfather was certainly an expert, but so was Brigadier Maxwell! She could well understand that it would be difficult to choose between the blooms that each of them grew.

'Er — we'd better have a pot of tea,' said the Brigadier awkwardly, as he asked her to sit down in the charming drawingroom. 'My daughter should have been here, but she won't be home till the weekend. She's working in Edinburgh at the moment.'

Shirley was looking at a beautiful portrait over the mantelpiece in the elegant room.

'That's Catriona,' the Brigadier said proudly. 'She's one of these beauty consultants. She gives advice on what to put on your face — not that you need it,' Brigadier Maxwell said hurriedly, so that Shirley smiled warmly for the first time. There was something rather nice about the old gentleman, an Edwardian courtesy.

She accepted a cup of tea as dark as treacle.

'Er — you're a doctor yourself, are you not?' he asked and saw the girl's face go white and rather drawn.

'Yes,' she said, her eyes downcast.

Always there was something to remind her of her job, and of the ordeal on Thursday evening which lay ahead.

She saw that Brigadier Maxwell was looking at her curiously and quickly came to the point.

'I believe you specialise in roses yourself,' she said, and he nodded.

'Beautiful flowers — exquisite. Your grandfather is trying for a scented white. I aim to get something a little more unusual — a blue rose. I've come close once or twice, but I haven't hit the bull's-eye yet!'

Shirley thought, privately, that she would not care for a blue rose.

'But they need attention,' she said quietly, 'and I just don't know what to do.'

The Brigadier's eyebrows seemed to

bristle and for a moment she felt a strange affinity with him. It was as though he, too, was being torn in two.

'I — I suppose I could help,' he said reluctantly, then seemed to be winning a battle with his better self.

'I'd *better* help. Dr Baxter has some — some fine roses.'

'I wouldn't bother you, but . . . '

'No,' he said, shaking his head. 'No, we mustn't let the bushes go. There's a lot of greenfly about. I'll come on Friday.'

'Oh, how kind of you,' Shirley said, feeling an immense relief. It was a problem which had worried her on and off for some time. 'Grandfather will be pleased and very grateful.'

Again the Brigadier flushed.

'I would rather you didn't tell him,' he said gruffly. 'No mention at all.'

'Oh, but . . . '

'No mention at all,' he repeated. 'That's my condition. He mustn't know I've touched his bushes. You understand?'

Shirley and he measured one another, and she nodded.

'Very well. Thank you, Brigadier.'

Walking away, Shirley pondered over the odd relationship which must exist between her grandfather and Brigadier Maxwell, then her thoughts went to Catriona.

She wondered where she had heard the name before, then remembered that Mrs Ross had referred to a girl with that name, with regard to Neil Fraser. Could it be the same girl, she wondered.

On Thursday afternoon, Shirley had little appetite for the substantial tea Mrs Ross had set before her. She had been upstairs to talk to her grandfather again, and had let it slip that she was due to take surgery this evening.

The old man's delight had made her heart sink, and now she was beginning to experience the familiar feeling of dread which had been with her in the last days at the hospital, before she handed in her notice.

Although the surgery was now quite familiar to her, it seemed once again alien to Shirley as she sat down and rang the bell for the first patient to be brought in.

She had hoped there would be only a handful of patients, but she soon began to see that her grandfather's practice covered a wide area, and several people were waiting.

*   *   *

The first few were easily dealt with, from a signature on a form to a prescription for a soothing lotion to relieve an irritating rash.

Then a young woman came in with a fretful baby boy, and Shirley looked in vain for notes on the baby's condition. Nervously, she examined the child, who cried with the pain of sickness, rather than the strong wail of temper.

The baby was sickening for something. But what? German measles? She slid her fingers over his body and round

53

the back of his neck, pressing gently, trying to make her diagnosis, though not entirely with confidence.

'How long has he been like this?' she asked the mother.

'Since yesterday, Doctor. He's been so fretful and off his food, then I noticed the rash. I — I got rather frightened . . . '

'It looks like German measles,' Shirley said, and the baby's mother looked at her anxiously.

'I was afraid of the rash,' she repeated.

'If you could give him this,' said Shirley, writing out a prescription, 'I'll come and see him again tomorrow.'

She had to trust her own judgment, she thought rather wildly, as her heart began to pound again. Suppose she was making a mistake! Suppose . . .

She swallowed, surprised to hear her own voice very steady as the young woman went out and she called for the next patient.

The next case was equally difficult, in

54

that Shirley had to question an elderly
man who was as unwilling to co-operate
as the baby!

'How often do you get the stomach
pains?' she asked. 'I mean, do you get
the pain when you've just eaten food, or
when your stomach is empty?'

'It goes away when I've had something to eat, Doctor,' the man told her,
and she made him lie down on the bed
while she examined the area where he
felt most pain.

'And how long since you noticed this
pain?'

'Oh . . . a while ago,' her patient said
vaguely. 'I didn't worry till it got bad.'

'When did it get bad?'

'Oh . . . a wee while now . . . '

Shirley was used to patients who
were vague over their own symptoms
and she examined him carefully, then
made notes, though already her mind
was forming a diagnosis.

Nervously she checked everything
again, coming to the same conclusion.
Her head ached as she wrote out a

prescription and said she would come to see the patient the following day. She would have to see Dr Andrews about this one.

'Is Dr Baxter nearly better?' the man asked. 'Will he be back in here soon?'

'No,' said Shirley, then smiled a little. 'But I, too, am Dr Baxter.'

There was no answering smile from her grandfather's patient.

Then, somehow, it was all over and the last patient seen out with a diet sheet in her handbag.

Shirley's mind went from the baby boy to the elderly man, and back again. Was she right? If she was wrong, would their condition worsen before other symptoms showed? Would valuable time be lost?

And Dr Andrews was in Inverness . . . Suddenly the door opened and Ian Andrews walked in. Shirley looked at him, and burst into tears.

Too Ambitious?

Shirley was aware of a look of surprise on Dr Andrews' face, followed by great concern as he came towards her. She had now given way to her tears, and was sobbing her heart out, her nerves jangled by the tension which had carried her through the whole surgery, increasing to breaking point now that it was all over.

'Dr Baxter! Shirley!' he said, coming to put an arm round her shoulders. His mind was registering the fact that the deep uneasiness he had felt about her while he was at the conference in Inverness was all too justified.

He had felt compelled to come and see if all was well with her, but now he could see that there was something badly wrong with Shirley Baxter, and that it was in some way tied in with her profession.

He reached over and grabbed a handful of large tissues from a box on the desk, handing them to her to wipe her tears.

'Get it over,' he said gently, 'then take a deep breath and tell me about it. There's something wrong, isn't there? With your career, I mean.'

Shirley nodded. Ian Andrews' perception had helped a little.

'Could you tell me about it?' he asked. 'Wait a moment, until you're calmer.'

'I — I'm sorry,' she said. 'It was such a strain. I — I felt that at any time I could make a terrible mistake . . .'

'You've made a mistake before?'

She nodded. 'More than one. That — that's why I decided not to practise any more. I — I've got another job waiting for me when Grandfather is better. I — I can't tell him now because he's going to be so disappointed . . .'

She choked again and a few hot tears trickled down her cheek.

'How did it happen?' Ian asked,

briskly matter-of-fact. 'Tell me from the beginning.'

In a strange way, it was cleansing to tell him all about her career. She gave him chapter and verse, and he stared at her musingly.

'Not so serious. These incidents could happen to any doctor, no matter how experienced. I wonder how many of us have to be pulled from the brink of disaster by someone when we are too tired to see it looming? It happened to a friend and myself when we were both young doctors, though rather in reverse,' Ian told her.

'I had checked on *him*, though it could so easily have been the reverse. Just think of that! If you'd been bright and fresh, you might have been the one to prevent a mistake, then you would be proud of yourself now, instead of miserable. There's always someone around to double check, isn't there? Soon your 'someone' will be yourself, a sort of inner instinct which tells you to look again, then again.'

Shirley was now silent, listening intently. She thought about the child she had seen, and the old man, Mr Elliott. Hadn't she experienced just this very thing when she was examining them, and hadn't she checked all her notes, then checked her own diagnosis again?

A moment later, she was telling Ian Andrews about the two cases, talking eagerly and competently.

'It seemed to be the first visit for both of them, though I think old Mr Elliott should have been to see you or Grandfather ages ago. He's been putting it off. It was his bad luck to get me, eventually, when he did take the plunge.'

'Maybe it was his good luck.' Ian grinned. '*I'm* the one who is having to watch out these days when sleep dulls the mind. I might have sent him home with a tablet, but now your diagnosis is going much deeper. Tell me again about it.'

Again Shirley's confidence grew as

she discussed the two cases with Dr Andrews, while he nodded quite often in agreement.

'It sounds to me as though you've done a splendid job,' he said, 'but I'll check on these cases and let you know what I think. There, does that make you feel better?'

Her eyes were shining with relief as much as tears. Shirley felt as though a load had been lifted from her shoulders, and that she could accomplish anything, while Dr Andrews was around to watch her do it!

'Oh, I feel better,' she told him. 'You don't know what you've done for me.'

For a moment, there was an odd expression in his eyes, then he grew brisk and matter-of-fact.

'Right. Well, I prescribe a good night's rest for both of us. I'll call on you again, if I may, to do another surgery for me. I'm sure you'll be able to do it without any trouble.'

He would have to build up her confidence, he thought, looking at her shrewdly, and it might take time. But he felt that the first step had been taken.

Slipping into bed that night, Shirley felt better than she had done in weeks, and most of her thoughts were full of Ian Andrews. How kind and dependable he was.

★   ★   ★

The following morning, Shirley was rather late out of bed, and as she pulled aside her curtain, she could see the snow-white head of Brigadier Maxwell bobbing up and down in the rose garden. Even as she looked, he pulled an old linen bonnet out of his pocket and clamped it down on his head, then bent to pick several leaves from the roses, examining them carefully.

Smiling, she ran down to the kitchen to drink a cup of scalding hot tea, then much refreshed, she made her way to Dr Baxter's room. The old man was awake, looking better again, though the days in bed were beginning to take their toll.

'I'll have to rub you down, Grandfather,' Shirley said, after the usual morning routine was accomplished.

'That's nurse's work,' he complained. 'Not for the likes of you. You've got better things to do, treating patients instead of nursing them better.'

'You're not any old patient, Grandfather.' She smiled. 'It's my privilege to nurse you.'

'How do you find young Andrews?'

Shirley turned a glowing face to him.

'Oh, he's the best,' she said. 'He's — he's really marvellous.'

Dr Baxter eyed her shrewdly, then frowned.

'Yes — well — he's a fine doctor.'

For a while, he asked her questions about patients he had known for years, and she asked him about old Mr Elliott, though Dr Baxter knew little about him professionally.

'He's a quiet man, clever with his hands, and always the same. He lost his wife a few years ago. Why do you want to know, lass?'

'Oh, no special reason.' she said hastily. 'I just like to know about people, that's all.'

'That shows the makings of a good doctor,' he said fondly. 'A good doctor treats people, the whole person, and not just his or her disease. Always keep interested in people, Shirley, and you can't go far wrong.'

His voice was growing weaker again, and she plumped up his pillows then made him rest.

She felt she must have a word with the Brigadier, just to acknowledge his presence and offer him a cup of coffee. It seemed rather off-hand to let him get on with it without acknowledging his presence.

Brigadier Maxwell accepted the mug of coffee gratefully, after refusing to come into the kitchen to drink it.

'No, I'd rather keep myself quiet here, among the roses,' he told Shirley when she went to find him. 'I don't want Hamish Baxter to hear me, and wonder what I'm doing here. Is his bedroom . . . ?'

Shirley had been wondering at the older man's slightly hoarse whisper, but now she smiled.

'On the other side of the house,' she said and Brigadier Maxwell looked relieved.

'See here . . . ' He broke off a rose leaf and handed it to her. She noted that it was discoloured and the texture poor.

'That shows what a week or two of neglect will do. It's a good job I came. There are pests on those bushes — greenfly — and they've already taken hold. I'm going to have to use my own special mixture to get control of it, and if your grandfather finds out, he'll have a relapse. Don't say I didn't warn you.

'He thinks that my mixture is a lot of rubbish, but I know of nothing better for this condition. Only, if we lose any, and he finds out, then my mixture will get the blame.'

Shirley nodded, hardly knowing what to say, though she wondered what sort of opinion her grandfather would give her of Brigadier Maxwell!

★ ★ ★

'So this is where you are!'

Suddenly a girl's voice startled her, and both she and the Brigadier whirled round to look at the beautiful girl who was coming towards them through the small gate, with Mrs Ross in hot pursuit.

'Miss Maxwell came, so — so I let her in,' she was saying.

'That's all right, Mrs Ross,' Shirley said quickly, and turned to watch the Brigadier greet his daughter.

There was nothing gruff about him now, and he turned, smiling, to introduce the two girls.

'This is my daughter, Catriona, Miss Baxter . . . Dr Baxter,' he corrected. 'You're home early, my dear.'

'Yes, I'm having a few days' holiday,

Father.' Catriona Maxwell said, then offered the tips of her fingers to Shirley.

'How do you do?'

Shirley acknowledged the introduction, thinking she had never seen a more beautiful girl, yet there was no warmth or friendliness in Catriona Maxwell's expression.

Her eyes surveyed Shirley coolly and with reserve.

'I was surprised to find you here, Father,' she said. 'I recognised the car.'

'Yes. I brought along a few things I thought I might need, my dear. Hamish Baxter is ill, you know, and his roses — well — we won't go into details.'

'If you've finished, then perhaps we can go home,' she said, and hastily he picked up some of his gardening equipment.

'Perhaps you two young ladies,' the Brigadier began, then saw that his daughter had no interest in prolonging the visit. 'Oh well, I'll see you later, Miss . . . Dr . . . I'll come back when I can.'

Shirley was still thinking about Catriona Maxwell that afternoon when she saw Neil Fraser coming up to the front door, a brown paper bag in his hand.

'I'll go, Mrs Ross.' she called as the bell shrilled, and hurried to let him in. She thought that he looked a bit tired as he turned to her when she opened the door.

'A bag of grapes for the invalid,' he said.

'Come in,' she invited. 'Grandfather is able to have visitors now. I know he'll be delighted to see you.'

'I can only spare a few minutes,' said Neil. 'The work on my new building project has been held up waiting for supplies. I must do some telephoning after four o'clock.'

'Ah, yes. It's some sort of sports complex, isn't it?'

She was unaware of the careful note in her voice, born of the various opinions and complaints she had heard from different people in Inverdorran, and Neil Fraser shot her a shrewd glance.

'Have you decided which side of the fence you're on?'

'Which . . . ?'

'Oh, come now, Dr Baxter — Shirley — you must be on either one side or the other. For, or against. I'm either ruining the place or bringing it some wealth. I'm either spoiling its beauty or saving it from dying of poverty.'

'I really haven't given it enough thought, Mr Fraser.'

'Neil.'

'Neil. It's none of my business.'

'Most people with any sort of interest in Inverdorran *make* it their business. Look, if you can spare a moment tomorrow afternoon, you could come out to the building site and I'll show you what it's all about. I'm not touting for support, but I'm fed up with people forming opinions without really going into details.'

'You mean people like Catriona Maxwell?' Shirley asked with sudden inspiration.

She had heard hints of a relationship between Neil and the lovely Maxwell girl, and now she felt, instinctively, that something had gone wrong, and it may be to do with this sports complex.

But if this was so, Neil Fraser had no intention of discussing it with her. Mention of Catriona Maxwell had taken all the warmth out of him and he looked at her stonily.

'What Catriona thinks is her own affair,' he said coldly. 'Nothing to do with me. Now, will you come and see my plans?'

'I'd like that very much,' Shirley said.

Old Dr Baxter was sitting up in bed and delighted to have a visitor.

Shirley left them to it while she helped Mrs Ross to prepare vegetables for the evening meal.

'Now who's at the door?' the older woman grumbled, as the bell shrilled again.

'I'll go,' Shirley said, wiping her hands.

This time it was Geoffrey Lewis, and

he needed no second invitation to come into the lounge.

'Hello, Dr Baxter,' he greeted her cheerfully. 'I'm back, as you see, and your car is safely back to the car hire firm.'

He fished in his pocket for a piece of paper.

'That's a relief,' Shirley said. 'It was costing me money. I hope you didn't have any trouble over it.'

'None whatsoever. Jock Sinclair checked it over for me before I left. Now let me see — here's the bill, and here's what I spent on it, plus my share of the hire for that day. Now do you agree with that amount?'

He and Shirley were bent over the figures when she heard the light footsteps of Neil running down the stairs. A moment later, he had walked into the lounge, the good humour on his face vanishing again as he recognised Geoffrey Lewis.

'Hello, Lewis,' he said coldly.

'Oh, it's you then, Fraser.'

Silently, they weighed up one another, and it was easy to see that real antagonism was beginning to brew up over the question of Neil Fraser's sports complex.

'I'll be off then, Shirley,' Neil said. 'See you tomorrow.'

'Very well. Around four. Now, Mr Lewis, I'll just write you a cheque.'

Geoffrey Lewis bit his lip. He was longing to know more about Shirley's date with Neil Fraser, but a look at her face kept him from asking questions. She was no ordinary girl, he thought, looking at her slight yet strong figure, and her unusual beauty.

'Thank you for seeing to the car,' she said, handing him the cheque.

That evening, Shirley's heart leapt when the telephone rang and Mrs Ross answered it, calling out that it was young Dr Andrews to speak to her.

'Hello — Shirley? Ian here. I've been to see the baby and it's certainly German measles.'

Shirley listened, smiling, thankful to

hear Ian's cheery voice. He always made her feel better.

'Don't worry about him. We'll have him better in no time. You did just fine. I've also been out to see old Mr Elliot. His cottage is out towards the Frasers' place . . .'

'Yes, I know,' she said, almost impatiently. 'What do you think, Ian?'

'I don't know,' he said carefully. 'I'm not easy about his condition at all, Shirley. I think we'll have to leave him a day or two to see what develops after he's had some of the pills I've given him.'

Shirley's heart sank. This time she had been wrong again, she thought, with sickening insight.

Her diagnosis was far from correct, but Ian didn't want to say so outright.

She could feel the old misery beginning to return.

'Hello? Shirley?'

'Yes, Ian, I'm here. It's all right,' she said quietly. 'I — I understand. You want to leave him for a day or two.'

'Yes. Are you all right?'

'Perfectly all right,' she said evenly. It was something she was going to have to learn to live with . . .

'OK. I'll see you another time.'

'Yes, of course.' She hung up and turned away, the feeling of brightness and keen interest in her job beginning to be over-shadowed with long, doubting fingers again.

★ ★ ★

The dull weather had brightened into pleasant sunshine the following day, and Shirley decided to walk out to Neil Fraser's place, hardly admitting to herself that she wanted to pass old Mr Elliott's cottage, and hoped to see him outside working in his garden or sitting on his summer seat.

The cottage was silent, however, and she passed by. The old man was Ian's responsibility now, not hers, yet she longed to know how he was progressing, and to see what new symptoms had developed which made nonsense of her own diagnosis.

She was still thinking of the old man when she reached the Fraser home, and was given a warm welcome by the other members of Neil's family. Jamie's sore knee was long since forgotten, but not the fact that she had given him prompt attention and had helped to heal the cut very quickly.

'You'll have tea with us, of course,' Mrs Fraser invited, admonishing her small son for making too much noise.

'Oh dear, I hope you'll excuse me,' Shirley said. 'I'm usually needed at home around tea-time. It's too much for Mrs Ross to manage on her own.'

'Then the quicker we get started, the better,' said Neil. 'Come on into my study, and have a look at some plans first of all.'

He had them all laid out for her on his desk, and pinned to a board on the wall. For a moment or two, Shirley could not make head nor tail of them, but as Neil began to explain each section, her interest was caught.

'When you take the size of the British Isles into account, I don't think anyone can claim we have too many sports complexes of this kind,' he said. 'Most families have to go to the Continent to enjoy the sort of things I'm going to offer, and I honestly believe I'm giving a service to people to help them enjoy their leisure in a healthy way.

'You should appreciate that, Shirley. They're going to be a great deal fitter after a holiday here at Inverdorran than sitting around with nothing to do. That creates boredom, and I'm sure half the young people who get into mischief do so because of boredom. I could create interest in sports which would last them for the rest of their lives.'

As she listened, Shirley wondered what had happened to the rather silent, taciturn young man she knew. Once started on his own subject, then Neil Fraser was never stuck for a word.

'Here we'll have swimming and ice-skating, and over here young lads will learn how to handle a boat properly, instead of risking life and limb in learning the hard way. There will be classes on climbing — and I don't need to tell you how important they will be — also horse riding, fencing, archery and the sort of set-up where we can drop something if it isn't a good proposition, and replace it with something else which is.

'There will also be amenities for the people who come, such as shops, etc., but designed into the whole scheme so that they don't look like bits added on.'

'What is that building marked with a cross?' she asked.

'That's the medical room. I plan to employ a doctor and a nurse. In fact, I was wondering . . . ' He hesitated then laughed and decided to take the plunge ' . . . if you would consider a job here.'

'I'm not practising medicine,' she said quickly.

'I hadn't forgotten.' For a moment, his eyes were speculative and his voice rather dry. 'This could be the sort of medicine you gave to Jamie. You didn't mind doing that.'

She was about to protest again, then she hesitated. 'I would have to think about it. Is that why you brought me here?'

'Not entirely,' he said coolly. 'I want you on my side.'

★ ★ ★

They had been walking around while she took in the work which had already been done. In spite of herself, she felt admiration stirring.

'It mustn't spoil Inverdorran,' she said, as they began to walk home.

'There's a lot of nonsense talked about that,' he said. 'Inverdorran is lovely, but not any more so than dozens of places in Scotland. If people just want to look at beauty, they can find plenty of other places. But how many of them can offer that beauty while also giving the kind of amenities I can offer?'

'It must be costing a lot,' she said, rather thoughtlessly, and this time he drew back rather coolly.

'Yes.' His voice was abrupt.

'I'm sorry. It isn't my affair.'

They rounded a corner, and suddenly all thoughts of the sports complex went out of Shirley's head as they came within sight of Mr Eliot's cottage. Outside the front door was an ambulance, its blue light flashing, and her heart leapt. What could have happened now, she wondered.

Emergency!

As Shirley and Neil Fraser caught sight of the ambulance outside old Mr Elliott's cottage, the young girl caught her breath, then broke into a run while Neil hurried along beside her.

'What's wrong with the old chap?' Neil was asking, but she could only shake her head. Even as they came within shouting distance, the ambulance took off, and Mrs Paterson, who lived next door, had turned to lock up the cottage.

'What — what has happened?' Shirley asked, trying to get her breath, as Martha Paterson turned towards them.

'Och, it's old Mr Elliott who isn't so well,' she said. 'He seems to be in a lot of pain. I had to get Dr Andrews.'

'And?' Neil prompted. His eyes were on Shirley's face, and he could see that the girl was very upset.

'I saw the milk still on the step,' Mrs Paterson was saying, 'so I knew there must be something wrong. He always brings it in first thing in the morning.'

Fleetingly, Shirley thought of the big London hospital and the cases she had dealt with there. If only neighbours had investigated more often when they saw the milk on the step, then how much easier her job might have been at times.

She smiled kindly to Mrs Paterson and thanked her for the information, but her eyes were full of worry as she turned again to Neil.

'I must go home now, Neil. Thank you for showing me the plans. We can talk about it another time, I'm sure.'

'Is everything OK?' he asked. 'Can't I help in any way?'

'No, everything is fine.' She smiled again, then a moment later she was hurrying up the road.

Shirley hurried to the telephone as soon as she reached Beech House, and dialled Ian's number, listening to the ringing noise as Mrs Ross crossed the hall. Slowly she put down the telephone.

'Is everything all right, Miss Shirley?' the woman asked, seeing her white face.

'Yes, fine. I'll go and sit with Grandfather now for a while before bedtime.'

At least there was peace and quiet in Beech House, she thought, as she sat in her grandfather's room, mending some bed linen, though her mind was far from peaceful as she went along to her own room an hour or two later. Just when she began to feel a small amount of confidence returning, something happened to destroy it.

Next morning, Shirley's nerves felt jangled and her one thought was to get hold of Ian and find out exactly how things stood. She knew he would be at the start of a very heavy day, but she hoped he wouldn't mind talking to her for a few moments.

She could hear the impatience in his voice, however, as he answered the telephone and she began to question him about the old man.

'I — I've been so worried,' she said.

'Take hold of yourself, Shirley,' he said. 'If there was anything really serious, I'd soon have got in touch with you, but the hospital can cope, you know.'

Swiftly Ian explained the circumstances.

'It was just as we thought,' he finished, 'an ulcer. So don't worry about him — he'll be OK. Is that all right, Shirley? I must go now because I'm snowed under with work.'

She heard him hang up, and replaced the receiver. It was all as she had suspected, but now she was full of doubt again. If Mrs Paterson had not noticed the milk, and Ian had not been available to get the old man to hospital, what would have happened? Should she have kept a much closer eye on him, knowing this sort of thing could happen?

Shirley's hands were trembling and

she dug her nails into her palms, taking hold of herself. Yet Ian had not blamed her in any way. He had treated her like a normal colleague, as he would have anyone else who had worked on the case with him. She sighed and relaxed a little. Somehow she felt that nothing very terrible would happen while Ian was around.

★ ★ ★

'Are you going upstairs, Miss Shirley?' Mrs Ross was asking as she crossed into the kitchen. 'Dr Baxter was wanting a jug of fresh water, and I've got it all ready for him. I'll take it up if you aren't going.'

'No, I'll take it,' Shirley said, smiling. 'He must be coming round now. He was still snoozing when I looked in a little while ago.'

'He's coming on by leaps and bounds now, Miss Shirley. He'll be on his feet one of these days, then we can all look out.'

Shirley grinned and Mrs Ross thought that the girl was looking better. She had not looked at all well the previous evening.

Dr Baxter was sitting up in bed leafing over the pages of a medical book when Shirley walked into the room and put fresh water and a glass on his bedside table.

'How some folk get off with writing books like this, I don't know,' he said. 'This man doesn't know what he's talking about.'

Shirley laughed. Last time it had been a book on roses she had found for him at the local library. That writer had not known what he was talking about either!

'What is it?' she asked.

'Children's diseases. He treats the disease all right, but not the child. I've seen the same thing in two different children, needing two different treatments, just because the children were as unlike one another as chalk and cheese. Why, I could tell you . . . '

He stopped, seeing that his granddaughter was standing in the middle of the room, staring into space. She seemed to do a lot of that. Either she was thinking about some young man, or else something was bothering her.

Dr Baxter frowned. He hoped she was not beginning to think too much about young Dr Andrews, though that was hardly likely. She seemed to have made friends with a doctor in London, and there was young Fraser, too. He was a good hard-working lad.

Dr Baxter wondered how to give Shirley the hint, but thought better of it. He should know by now never to interfere with the affairs of young people. If he'd been a bit more tolerant with Colin, Shirley's father, then how different things might be now!

Thinking of Colin, Dr Baxter wondered if Shirley had had a letter recently. It seemed a while since he had heard, himself.

'Have you had a letter from your mother or father?' he asked.

'Pardon?' Shirley asked absent-mindedly.

'Your mother — have you heard?'

'Not since that air letter, though I expect Mum is busy with Dad having to lie on his back.'

'On his back? What do you mean, Shirley?'

Too late Shirley realised she had spoken thoughtlessly. Her father's accident with the tractor had not been too serious, but it was going to mean quite a few weeks on his back, before he was well enough to carry on. Doing hard physical work meant that his body had to be strong, and he could not take chances. It was going to mean a patient wait.

Now old Dr Baxter was staring at her, his eyes wide with anxiety.

'You aren't telling me the whole truth, Shirley. I could feel you hiding something from me, ever since you've come here. There's something up, and I want to know what it is.'

'Don't get excited, Grandfather,' she soothed. 'I'll tell you exactly what it is, then you'll understand. Dad *has* had an accident, but he's finding it a lot more of a nuisance than anything else.'

As clearly as possible, she told her grandfather all about her father's accident with the tractor, and the old man nodded a few times.

'Poor Colin,' he said, leaning back. 'You should have told me.'

'It would just have been one more thing for you to worry about.'

'What's happening to his work then?'

'Oh, Paul can cope. He's only nineteen, and Nancy sixteen, but they love the farm. They take after Mother's side and are born farmers, whereas I . . .'

'You're a born doctor,' her grandfather said fondly. 'It's funny how it keeps coming out in the blood.'

Shirley said nothing, though she coloured uncomfortably.

'Anyway, I'm glad I know what's been on your mind,' old Dr Baxter said, and she still made no reply. She had thought she'd been making a good job of hiding her problems, but it seemed that this had not been the case.

'When Father feels better, I'm sure he'll be on the first available plane to come and see you,' she said, and the old man's face lit up.

'Do you think so, Shirley?'

'He's often said he would like to come home and see you, but always something has cropped up. Farming is just as demanding as medicine, you know, Grandfather.'

'I believe you,' the old man said.

He was looking a bit tired after his small bout of excitement, and now he lay back on the pillows, his pale eyes bright with pleasure.

'It makes you think, though, Shirley. I've always felt in my heart that Colin will come home one day, but if this accident had been worse, then I might never have seen him again. And all due to careless words and stubborn natures. It makes you think . . . '

'Don't worry about it,' Shirley urged. 'We'll get a letter soon, you'll see.'

'No, I won't worry, lass.'

Yet the shock had taken its toll and

the old man was glad to shut his eyes for a few minutes. Shirley looked at him a trifle anxiously, then decided to leave him alone. The worst thing she could do for her grandfather was to fuss about him like a mother hen.

★ ★ ★

She remembered that Mrs Ross had wanted her to do some shopping, and it might be needed by lunchtime. Quietly she went downstairs and collected the shopping list and the large wicker basket.

'I shan't be long, Mrs Ross,' she said. 'Grandfather will probably have a nap. Oh, he knows now about — about Father's accident.'

'Oh, I'm glad,' Mrs Ross said. 'I was afraid that any day I would let the cat out of the bag.'

'No, that was left to me.' Shirley smiled rather ruefully, as she turned away.

Shirley liked doing the shopping for

Mrs Ross, even though the choice was usually take it or leave it, and if she needed anything out of the ordinary run of things, then Hannah McEwan was inclined to shake her head rather soulfully and tell Shirley there was 'no call for it.'

It was happening now over a packet of curry powder. Shirley had learned to enjoy a nice curry now and again when Brian Wills had taken her to a small Indian restaurant near the hospital in London. Now she planned to cook one for herself.

'Don't go giving the doctor any,' Mrs Ross had said as she added the curry powder and long-grained rice to her shopping list.

'Oh, Mrs Ross!' Shirley laughed. 'You'd think I was planning to poison him.'

Now she had managed to buy the rice quite easily, but not the curry powder, and for a moment she fought down her annoyance. She loved Inverdorran as it was, with all its peace and quiet, but now and again she had a sneaking sympathy for Neil Fraser and his sports complex.

Perhaps the General Stores might even be tempted to stock curry powder, if they had a few more people making a call on it.

'I would have thought that other people besides myself would have asked for such a thing,' she said.

'We usually shop for extras like this in Glasgow,' said a voice behind her, and she turned round to see Catriona Maxwell looking at her, her eyes full of amusement.

'Hannah would have to carry a big stock she could not afford if she had to cater for everyone's tastes.'

'That's right, Miss Maxwell,' Hannah said. 'It's a job to keep up the ordinary stock as it is.'

'Sorry,' Shirley said contritely. 'I'll remember next time I go to town. What about tea?'

'Indian or China?' Hannah asked, and both girls laughed heartily.

The small incident in the General Stores seemed to have softened up Catriona Maxwell, Shirley thought, as the girl asked her to wait for her since she had a few more purchases.

'We can walk towards Beech House together, if you like,' she suggested. 'As a matter of fact, Father asked me to pick up a bottle of rose fertiliser on the way past.'

'Of course. I'll be glad to wait,' Shirley said.

Catriona was still as beautiful and well groomed as ever, she thought, looking at her stylish skirt and sweater, her hair beautifully brushed, and caught back by a matching headband. She made Shirley feel she could have spent a little more time on her own appearance.

* * *

'It's very good of Brigadier Maxwell to help out in this way, with Grandfather's roses,' Shirley said, as she and Catriona swung into step together.

'Oh, he's enjoying it, really,' the other girl said. 'He's always out examining cuttings and there isn't enough to keep him busy among his own stock in summertime. He's glad of something extra to do.'

'Grandfather is aiming for a pure white rose,' Shirley said, after they had walked on in silence for a little while. She had a feeling that Catriona wanted to say something to her, but didn't quite know how to start.

'I thought there were already dozens of pure white roses,' Catriona said.

'I think there are ones almost white, but it must be pure,' Shirley suggested, and Catriona shrugged.

'Oh well, you obviously know more about it than I do.' She then paused and gave Shirley a sideways glance. 'I — er — I saw you walking around the new sports complex with Neil.'

So it was Neil Fraser, thought Shirley!

'Yes?' she asked, carefully.

94

'I — well, I was wondering if you found it interesting.'

'Oh yes, very interesting. It's a fine project.'

Again there was heavy silence between them as they walked along, and Shirley could almost feel the impatience in the other girl. She was longing to ask a great many questions, Shirley knew, but she didn't feel it was her business to discuss the sports complex with Catriona Maxwell.

'Geoffrey Lewis thinks it will spoil the place,' Catriona said. 'He's hard at work getting up some sort of petition. I'm bound to think he's got a point, and I could easily agree with him.'

'Neil has a point of view as well,' Shirley said, 'and I think it's a good one.'

'Then you side with Neil Fraser?' Catriona's new friendly approach began to wear a bit thin. 'That's just like a newcomer who hasn't yet got the feel of the place.'

'As you say, I'm a newcomer,' Shirley

said quietly, 'and as such, I've no desire to take sides. I don't think it would be a bad thing, though, if someone as enterprising as Neil Fraser and his brother brought a little prosperity to Inverdorran.

'And I'd rather see it all developed by someone who lives here, and cares about it all, than a perfect stranger who doesn't care about Inverdorran at all. That has happened to some places in the past.'

'Then he's definitely going ahead?' Catriona asked. 'I mean — there's no turning back now? I know the site is being cleared, but has he got the backing he needs?'

Shirley stared at her. Catriona must have a very special interest in what Neil was doing or she would never have asked such a question. Yet if she cared deeply for Neil, surely she would be supporting him in what he was trying to do.

'I think Neil is the person you should be asking, not me,' she said.

'But surely you must have formed some sort of idea, walking round with him as you did, and having all sorts of things pointed out to you.'

'I still think you should discuss it with Neil, since it matters to you so much,' Shirley insisted, and Catriona looked taken aback, then seemed to pull herself together.

'Yes, I'm sorry,' she said, then something of her stiff, haughty attitude began to return. 'I just find things which affect Inverdorran of absorbing interest, since my home is here.'

She managed to make Shirley feel an outsider again.

'I'll get the rose fertiliser for you,' she said. 'Perhaps Mrs Ross has put it somewhere.'

Catriona took it with a word of thanks, then strode away.

★ ★ ★

'Dr Andrews has been in asking for you,' Mrs Ross said, as Shirley began to unpack her shopping basket.

'He thinks that Dr Baxter should stay in bed a day or two yet before attempting to get up, and he said that he may look in and see you later.'

'Oh dear, I'm sorry I've missed him.' Shirley was surprised at her own disappointment. Somehow it always helped a great deal even to talk to Ian.

'Where is he now?' she asked.

'That's what I was going to tell you. You know Camusling, that wee hamlet farther up the valley?'

Shirley shook her head. There was a great deal of territory she still didn't know.

Mrs Ross went on to explain.

'It's part of Dr Baxter's practice, and there's a young couple up there with four children. The man works at the Forestry, and three of the children go to school. The bus picks them up each day. But the wee one seems to have taken ill. I heard Dr Andrews asking Mrs Graham a lot of questions on the phone, and it was to do with a rash.'

'A rash?'

'Ay, it's a rash that's bothering him. Dr Andrews went off in a hurry.'

Yes, he would, Shirley thought, nodding.

'I didn't get the curry powder,' she said.

Mrs Ross grinned.

Shirley had just removed her jacket, when the telephone shrilled again.

'I'll get it,' she called to Mrs Ross, wondering if she would hear Ian's voice, but it was the deep, measured tones of Neil Fraser.

'Hello, Shirley. Is Dr Andrews with you? I've been trying to reach him everywhere.'

'No, he's gone up the valley to a place called Camusling.'

'Oh, no!'

She could hear his rather heavy, laboured breathing and quite a lot of noise and shouting in the background.

'What is it, Neil?' she asked anxiously.

'An accident. I'm at the sports

complex. Look, Shirley, you're a doctor. Can you come now?'

The familiar feeling of clamming up was with her again, and Shirley found she was shaking her head.

'Oh, Neil, I — I . . . '

'I know it's no job for a girl. A man is trapped under a fall of masonry, and he seems to be in terrible pain. He could do with something — an injection probably — to help him, and he certainly needs an ambulance. And although you *are* just a girl, you're a doctor, too, aren't you?'

'Yes,' she said, huskily.

'And presumably you wouldn't have chosen the profession if you weren't prepared to face unpleasant tasks like these.'

'I'll be along as quickly as I can,' she assured him. 'Just let me find my bag.'

Pulling herself together, she got out her grandfather's car and drove down to the sports complex.

As she got out of the car, Geoffrey Lewis hurried towards her.

'I saw it all,' he said. 'I'm going to report this to the authorities. If there was proper planning, accidents like this wouldn't happen. That man there, is . . . '

'Please, Mr Lewis, I must hurry,' she said firmly.

'It's no place for a young girl like you. There's another wall, there, which could go at any time, and if Fraser doesn't watch out, fire could easily break out. There could be gas . . . '

'Mr Lewis, I think you'd better go home,' Shirley said, her cheeks flushing with annoyance.

Yet she felt she ought to be grateful to Geoffrey Lewis. The anger had chased away the last of her doubts and fears, and her one thought now was for the man involved in the accident.

A crowd of people had gathered and as she fought her way forward, it seemed that the whole of Inverdorran had turned up at the building site.

'Please let me through — I'm a doctor,' she was saying.

Suddenly, Neil Fraser was in front of her, his face blackened and his eyes wild with worry and impatience. Quickly, he took hold of her hands.

'Where have you been?' he asked, his voice shaking with nerves. 'Over here, if you're going to do anything to help this man.'

Who Was Miss Alison?

Shirley looked at the people standing around at the building site, and would have liked to send them all away. In other circumstances, they might have made her nervous, but there was no time for that as she followed Neil Fraser towards the man who lay trapped under the debris.

Kneeling down, she examined him quickly and expertly, then looked up at Neil, who was trembling with agitation.

'Have you telephoned for an ambulance, Neil?' she asked quietly, and he seemed to pull himself together.

'I'll do that straightaway.'

Having something to do seemed to ease the strain on Neil Fraser, and he strode about, uttering crisp orders, while Shirley gave some much-needed first-aid.

The man was badly injured about the

head, and quickly she assessed his requirements for when he reached hospital. It might be helpful for the doctor in charge.

She worked easily and methodically, unaware of the eyes looking on, and the people who viewed her efforts with some relief. There was no doubt now that the girl was indeed Dr Baxter's granddaughter, and was likely to be as clever and capable as the old man.

Yet each minute began to seem like an hour to her, after she had done all she could.

'What is his name?' she asked Neil.

'Walter Maguire.'

'You'll have to inform his family. There will be papers to sign at the hospital.'

'That has already been done,' Neil said rather harshly. 'By the schoolmaster, Mr Lewis.'

'Oh.' She looked round quickly, remembering how Geoffrey Lewis had waylaid her as she was coming to attend to the injured man. He had claimed that the site was unsafe, and now she wondered if he was right.

'I should ask everyone to go home,' she suggested.

'They'll go — after the ambulance has disappeared out of sight. Mrs Maguire was away visiting a friend, and she'll be here shortly. I hope she has the sense to leave the children with a neighbour.'

Shirley's fingers were on Walter Maguire's pulse. She seemed to have been kneeling there for hours and wondered how long, indeed, the man had lain there, injured. He needed hospital treatment urgently.

Then suddenly, everything was happening as Mrs Maguire arrived, brought to the site by Geoffrey Lewis, and with a tremendous sense of relief, Shirley also saw that the ambulance was arriving.

Mrs Maguire was weeping.

'Will you come with us, Doctor?' she asked. 'Please? It's a few miles to the hospital and — and I'd feel better.'

'All right,' Shirley agreed, smiling reassuringly, taking the older woman's hand.

Again it seemed a long, nightmare drive, but Shirley felt that Walter Maguire was holding his own. Her emergency treatment seemed to be having good effect.

She had a few, quick words with the casualty staff as the injured man was carried in, giving them a sample of blood for the Pathological Laboratory to save time, and helping Mrs Maguire with all she had to do.

Together they waited to hear that Walter Maguire had had an emergency operation to relieve pressure on his head, and although his back was injured, no bones were broken.

'We can only wait now — and pray,' Shirley said quietly to Mrs Maguire. 'We'd better go home and the hospital will get in touch if they need you.'

It was only when they walked out of hospital that Shirley realised they had no transport, but a moment later a tall, lean figure loomed up.

'How is he?' Neil asked. 'I — I've brought the car. I knew you would have no means of getting home.'

'He's being well looked after. He'll be out of commission for a while, but the chances are he'll pull through without lasting damage,' Shirley told him.

She looked at Mrs Maguire, who was white and tired.

'We'll have you home in no time, Mrs Maguire,' Neil said gently, but the woman made no reply, and Shirley could sense her hostility towards Neil.

In silence, they drove back to Inverdorran.

★   ★   ★

Next morning, Shirley got out of bed with a sense of purpose. She was remembering Neil Fraser's white face, and the measures she had taken to counteract the shock of it all, both for him and Mrs Maguire. She telephoned the hospital, and was told that her patient was as well as could be expected, and was comfortable.

Breathing a sigh of relief, she collected her bag and got out her grandfather's old car to drive over to the Frasers' farm. She calculated that the family would still be at breakfast, but she wanted to see Neil before he went off to work. She was not at all sure that he was well enough to undertake any duties today, but he was the type to drive himself on.

When Shirley arrived he was drinking a cup of coffee, having no appetite for food.

'I'll have a cup of that, too.' She smiled, then turned to look closely at Neil, seeing the signs of strain on his face.

'You should be resting in bed today, Neil.'

'No way,' he told her. 'I've got quite a lot of sorting out to do.'

'Geoffrey Lewis says the site isn't safe,' she said. 'Can't someone else look into that for you, in case?'

'Geoffrey Lewis knew nothing about it,' he told her roughly.

'But a man has been injured! He could have been killed.'

'A man who completely disregarded all the safety regulations laid down. He wore his helmet for five minutes, then as soon as my eyes were off him, he took it off. I warned him about it, and if he had not been married with children, I would have sacked him. I suppose that therein lies any blame — the fact that I *didn't* sack him. He might have been better off today.'

'But he was a mature man. He should have seen the wisdom of following safety measures.'

'Yes,' Neil agreed heavily. 'He should.'

There was silence until Shirley turned again to Neil.

'Nevertheless, you've got yourself to think about, too. It's all been a bit of a strain for you.'

'It won't be any less of a strain stuck at home brooding over it. No, I've got to get on the job. Anyway, your pills have sorted me out, Doctor!'

She grinned, pleased to see a hint of lightness in his manner. It was odd, but she really did feel like a doctor again. She hadn't had to stop and consider any part of the treatment she had given. It had all been done with swift certainty, just like the old days.

'Call me if you feel off-colour at all then, Neil,' she said, as she picked up her bag and glanced at her watch.

Ian would be doing morning surgery, but he would call in later to see her. Suddenly her heart was full of joy at the thought, and her whole being lit up with happiness.

She turned a glowing face to Neil Fraser, who looked at her silently, thinking he had never seen anyone quite so lovely, yet knowing that her inner radiance had nothing to do with him.

'Thanks for all you've done, Shirley,' he said, awkwardly.

'I'm glad to have been of help,' she

said and he couldn't doubt her
sincerity.

★　★　★

Back home, Shirley found her grandfather sitting up in bed after his
breakfast.

'I've been out doing some work,' she
told him cheerfully. 'Do you feel well
enough to sit out on your chair again,
Grandfather? Think how nice it will be
to tell Ian you're so much better when
he comes to see you.'

'Why not?' the old man asked, his
eyes resting on her shining face. 'You
seem to enjoy being back in harness
again.'

'Yes, I am,' she said confidently, and
began to tell him about Walter Maguire's
accident, going into technical details,
which he grasped straightaway, judging
by his shrewd questions and her swift
replies.

'I know the Maguires,' he said slowly.
'She's a quiet little soul, but he's a bit

of a fool. I could imagine that he wouldn't want to be bothered with a helmet or gloves. And poor Neil will have to bear the brunt.'

But Shirley had put Neil Fraser to the back of her mind as she changed into a pretty dress that afternoon, and combed out her hair, which now fell in soft waves to her shoulders. She was looking her best, she thought happily. The fresh air of Inverdorran had done wonders for her complexion and there was a soft glow in her cheeks.

Ian turned up in time to drink a cup of tea with her in the afternoon. She didn't miss his start of surprise at the sight of her, used as he was to seeing her in slacks or a skirt with a plain sweater. The dress did wonders for her appearance.

'Come in, Ian,' she said, smiling. 'Grandfather is a lot better today and . . . '

'It looks as though it's taken a load off your mind, too, Shirley,' he said, smiling.

'Yes, it has. Did you hear about the accident up at the Fraser building site?'

His face sobered as he accepted a cup of tea.

'Did I not! The place is buzzing with it. I hear you've fairly proved yourself as the other Dr Baxter over it, anyway.'

She laughed and coloured. 'I felt a great deal more confident over it than I've done for ages, thanks to you,' she added softly.

'Now, don't go saying things like that,' Ian said, putting his cup down. 'I take no credit at all for helping to do something which time would have done anyway.'

'Oh, but you don't know . . . ' she began, and he laughed lightly.

'Oh, but I do! You're grateful to me because you think I've helped you, but there's no need, Shirley. It has happened to a great many of us, but we all come round, one way or another. Did you hear about that wee boy up at Camusling?'

The smile had left Shirley's eyes as

she stared at Ian thoughtfully. It was almost as though he were mentally backing away from her. Then she felt that he understood. She had known other doctors like him in hospital, who hated to be thanked for performing near miracles.

What a wonderful person he was, she thought, her eyes glowing, and how much she was coming to care for him. He was so quiet and unassuming, wanting nothing for himself, yet how much one could come to depend on him.

'Did you hear about the child?' he was asking, and she pulled herself together.

'Oh — oh, yes. He has a rash, hasn't he?'

'I think we run the risk of having measles on our hands.'

'But surely, with vaccination . . . '

'Some enlightened parents, but not all. There will still be enough to keep us — me — busy.'

'Us,' she corrected. 'Ian, I can help you now, really I can. I'll do surgery for you any time you have a lot of work on your hands.'

Even as she said it, she could see his fatigue as though he was only keeping going with superhuman effort.

'Oh, Shirley, that would be wonderful — a great help.'

'Of course I'll do it,' she said gently. 'Surgery tomorrow?'

For Ian, she was prepared to work till she dropped!

The hours seemed to fly past the following morning as Shirley took surgery for Ian.

★ ★ ★

Later, she had finished her meal and was drinking a cup of coffee in her grandfather's room, eagerly talking over her cases, when Mrs Ross came to find her.

'That Mr Lewis, the schoolteacher, would like a word with you, Miss Shirley,' she said. 'He's in the sitting-room.'

'Oh, bother,' Shirley said, and caught a twinkle in her grandfather's eyes. He could well imagine that a few young men would like a word with Shirley!

'I'll be back to help you sit out in your chair, just as soon as he has gone,' she promised.

Downstairs, Geoffrey Lewis leapt to his feet eagerly when Shirley walked into the room.

'Hello, Mr Lewis,' she said, and he coloured, his eyes on her admiringly.

'Oh, won't Geoffrey do?'

She always forgot, she thought, nodding as she invited him to sit down. He was such an earnest young man, but they seemed to have nothing in common.

'It's about Patsy and Tommy,' he began.

'Patsy and Tommy?'

'Maguire. They're two of my pupils. It was their father who was so badly injured on that eyesore of a building site. Poor things, with their father at death's door . . .'

'What can I do for them?' Shirley asked.

'You can be a witness,' he told her eagerly, 'to say Walter Maguire is so badly injured, he might have lost his life. I'm making a complaint to the authorities on behalf of Mrs Maguire, and your evidence could be of great importance. Now, I've drafted it all out.'

He dived into a briefcase and brought out a sheaf of papers.

'All you have to do is sign your name here, if you agree with all I've said. I'll leave it for you to read, and come back this evening.'

'Mr Lewis! Geoffrey!' she said. 'Please don't! I don't wish to sign anything of the kind. I'm quite sure there is going to be an official enquiry and I'll be called as a witness. I can only verify that Walter Maguire was injured. I can't say anything about the circumstances, or — or anything else. So if you don't mind, I'll wait for that enquiry.'

'But these things take time,' he argued. 'By then we don't know what else may have happened.'

'I'm sure there won't be a repeat accident. They will all have learned their lesson.'

'And I'm sure the situation calls for someone with a bit of strength of character to speak out,' Geoffrey said, standing up. 'Well, maybe I don't need your signature. Perhaps I'll manage without.'

He thrust the papers back into his briefcase and turned to look at her, his cheeks flushed.

'I hope you won't regret your lack of co-operation, Shirley — Doctor . . . '

'I hope not,' she said quietly, and shut the door behind him.

Slowly, she climbed the stairs to her grandfather's bedroom, but this time she didn't discuss her problem. The old man was making progress, but it must be done very slowly.

★ ★ ★

118

Old Dr Baxter was able to sit by an open window as the weather had warmed to a true summer's day, with hardly a soft breeze to stir the leaves. He sat enjoying the fresh air, and the scent of flowers, as Shirley made his bed and plumped up his pillows.

'Mr Lewis didn't stay long,' her grandfather said probingly.

'No,' Shirley answered shortly, then smiled a little. 'Nothing to worry about, Grandfather.'

Yet she could see by his eyes that he was aware of her disquiet. Perhaps it would do more harm to leave him in the dark.

'He wants to make trouble for Neil Fraser over that accident,' she said. 'He feels that Neil is out to spoil the beauty of the countryside.'

'Don't let him,' old Dr Baxter said. 'Neil is a good lad. He's trying to do something very worthwhile.'

'Then you approve?'

'Of course I do. Oh, I admit I had my doubts at first, but Neil loves Inverdorran as much as anybody, and will see that only good comes of his sports complex. He will see that the whole thing is planned with good taste, and it will provide a lot of work for local people.

'We could do with more young men with his imagination and courage these days, willing to take a chance, and not sparing themselves.'

'That's true,' Shirley said thoughtfully.

It certainly must take courage to start such an enterprise.

Her grandfather had leaned out of the window and was looking down at his rose garden.

'Why, Shirley!' he cried. 'I expected my roses to be almost ruined with neglect, yet just look at them!'

He turned to look at his granddaughter wonderingly.

'They're in as good shape as I've managed myself! You must have inherited green fingers, my dear, and a real way with roses. I've never seen them looking better.'

Shirley swallowed, her face scarlet. She had been hoping to break it gently to her grandfather that Brigadier Maxwell was still coming in to see to the flowers, but so far she had not managed to raise the subject.

Even as she drew breath, the old man suddenly leaned out again, and both of them watched as the Brigadier walked quietly into the rose garden from the side gate, carrying a sprayer.

'Maxwell?' Dr Baxter said. 'What's he doing here?' He turned to her, his eyes flashing angrily. 'What's he doing here, Shirley?'

'Well, Grandfather . . . ' She broke off as the colour began to drain from the old man's cheeks.

'Oh dear, I — I . . . ' he began.

'Do you feel ill, Grandfather?'

The old man nodded and Shirley helped him back into bed, hurrying to give him one of his pills. She sat by the side of the bed, feeling very anxious, but soon Dr Baxter's breathing became easier and he dropped off to sleep.

Going downstairs quietly, Shirley picked up the telephone and dialled Ian's number. It was Mrs White, Ian's housekeeper, who answered.

'Oh, it's you, Dr Shirley,' she said.

'Yes, Mrs White. Is Dr Andrews in?'

'No, I'm sorry, he's just slipped out on an errand. We've got Miss Alison coming on a short visit, you see. I'll tell him you called, Dr Shirley.'

'Thank you.' Shirley put down the telephone, her eyes puzzled. Who was Miss Alison? It was funny that she knew so little about Ian's family. He never mentioned his parents. Could it be that he only had a sister?

Mrs Ross would know, she thought, as she made for the kitchen, then she paused as the front doorbell shrilled loudly.

Crossing the hall, she opened the door to find Neil on the doorstep, his face like thunder. He strode in without invitation.

'Why, Neil! Is anything wrong?' she asked.

'Wrong? Of course there's something wrong,' he told her angrily. 'I understand you're going as a witness for Walter Maguire against me at the enquiry over the accident at the sports complex. That's what is wrong, Shirley.'

Ready To Tackle Anything

Shirley stared at Neil as he glared at her angrily, a nerve twitching at the side of his mouth. What on earth was he talking about?

'Please come in, Neil,' she invited.

'This isn't a social call, Shirley,' he said. 'I feel . . . '

'In here, Neil. And try to calm down, for goodness' sake. All that shouting will upset Grandfather. Now tell me again what you said . . . That I'm going as — a witness?'

'As if you didn't know!' he said.

He had refused her offer of a chair in the sitting-room and now he paced up and down, though she could sense the tension in him and knew that he was more upset than angry.

'Just what makes you accuse me of acting against you, Neil?'

He turned to face her. 'I've been to

see Mrs Maguire and, as you probably know, our friend, Mr Lewis, is always in and out of that house. He told her that she needn't worry about a thing since you would be a witness against me.

'You can't deny that he has been here to see you, Shirley. I saw him leaving with a briefcase, pushing some papers into it. I didn't think anything of it at the time . . .'

'And now you've put two and two together to make four!'

'Was he here, and did he ask you to go as witness for him?'

'Yes, but . . .'

'I thought so,' Neil said. The colour was high in his cheeks, and she saw that he was too distraught to listen to explanations.

'I won't discuss it till you calm down,' she said firmly.

Neil looked at her flushed cheeks, then he strode towards the door.

'I thought you understood, Shirley,' he said, 'but I see now I was wrong. Don't worry, though, I'll manage to work things out in my own way, even if the whole of Inverdorran is against me! I know what I'm doing, and none of you will put me off!'

'But, Neil!' She wanted to tell him that she was far from being against him, but he strode to the front door, let himself out and closed it firmly.

Mrs Ross had come into the hall from the kitchen, carrying a tray set for tea.

'Och, I was just bringing tea for you and Mr Fraser, Miss Shirley. Is he away?'

Shirley swallowed and nodded. 'Yes, he's just gone.'

'Well, never mind. Maybe you'll be glad of a cup yourself, though young Mr Fraser shouldn't go rushing about the way he does. He'll wear himself out before that sports place gets under way.'

'If it ever does,' Shirley said dismally.

'Well, it should if he is due any reward for all the hard work he's putting in. I think a lot of folk see that now, and admire him for it. And he does right by his employees, too. He keeps paying the Maguires while Walter is in hospital, and Hannah McEwan was saying it was out of his own pocket.'

'How you all gossip!' Shirley said, feeling that she wanted to cry.

Mrs Ross stopped in mid-flow, looking rather offended.

'I'm sorry. We just take an interest in one another, Miss Shirley,' she said.

'I'm the one to be sorry,' Shirley said, rather wearily. 'I was just a bit upset about Mr Fraser. As you say, he could do with relaxing a bit.' She felt disturbed by the memory of the way Neil had looked at her, almost with contempt added to his anger.

Now she could understand a little better. He was supporting the Maguires, yet here they were, hoping for large sums in compensation, enough to damage or even ruin Neil's project, and he thought she was willing to be a party to it.

Maybe, when he thought about it, he would realise how wrong he was. Yet she had not done much to reassure him. She should have denied it straightaway, but she had been taken by surprise.

Slowly, she made her way up to her grandfather's room. He was taking things quietly again, with good sense, knowing that to hurry his recovery just meant a setback for a few days. Now he was sleeping, and Shirley went to the window, gazing down on the rose beds.

She had better see Brigadier Maxwell and ask him not to come again. It was better for the roses to be a little bit neglected, than for her grandfather to be upset by having his rival attend to them.

She had not realised he would object so strongly, and privately thought he was being a bit childish! Then she remembered that he was getting on in years, and was weakened by his illness. Patients often allowed small things to upset them, things they could have taken in their stride under normal circumstances.

★ ★ ★

The following afternoon, Shirley set out for the Maxwell house shortly after lunch.

She had been busy that morning helping Ian with morning surgery, and it was a measure of her new-found confidence that she had coped with each case with absorbed interest and complete certainty, so that she felt stimulated rather than fatigued after she had eaten her lunch.

Gradually she was getting to know a great many people in Inverdorran, and now felt very much at home in the place.

She thought about her own home in New Zealand, and particularly about her father. The news was good from her own folk now, and sometimes she felt very homesick when she thought of them all, her parents, brother and sister, picturing what they would be doing at any particular hour of the day.

She came out of her reverie as she

realised that she was now outside the Maxwell home. Quickly she opened the gate and walked up to the front door. From somewhere within the house she could hear the doorbell shrilling, but after a second ring, she knew there was no-one at home and turned away reluctantly. It would have been nice to resolve this question of the roses with Brigadier Maxwell now, and not allow it to drift.

Shirley walked away, sticking her hands deep into her pockets as she turned back towards Beech House. She glanced round quickly before crossing the road, and suddenly caught sight of Catriona Maxwell walking along from the opposite direction.

Shirley paused thankfully. She would still have to see the Brigadier, but at least she could leave a message with Catriona. Then her eyes went to the tall figure striding beside Catriona, and she recognised Neil Fraser.

Slowly, Shirley wandered on in the shadow of the hedges which lined the paths. Catriona and Neil were talking so earnestly that she hesitated to walk towards them. She had the curious feeling that her presence would be an intrusion.

She found she was looking at Neil with a professional eye, at the tension in him, and the way he ran a hand through his hair.

Slowly, Shirley walked on, feeling uneasy and disturbed about Neil. She hoped Catriona Maxwell was not adding to the pressures which were already laid on him.

* * *

Before surgery that evening, Ian called in, just to check up on Dr Baxter. He was looking so much brighter and more energetic himself, Shirley felt a renewed thrill that she could now take quite a few cases off his hands. He greeted her with a glowing face and radiant smile.

'My word, Ian, you do look better,' she said, delighted to see him.

'I feel it. A few good nights' sleep can do wonders for a chap. And how are you? You must be pleased to see how well your grandfather is coming on. Personally, I'll be delighted to see him back on his feet, and there's no reason why he shouldn't be, fairly soon. His heart isn't at all bad for a man of his age. He's been sorely missed around the village.'

'That's what I've been telling him,' Shirley agreed. 'I think he's been greatly helped by the affection which people have shown for him.'

'He's earned it,' said Ian.

Shirley's private thoughts were that Ian had also earned himself a similar place. On her last visit to Inverness, she had seen a lovely little desk clock in a jeweller's window, and thought how suitable it would be for Ian's big desk. It would be less trouble than continually glancing up at the wall clock.

With only a moment's thought, Shirley had popped into the shop and had bought the gift for Ian, asking the assistant to gift-wrap it. Now she excused herself and went over to her grandfather's old wall cupboard and took out the gift, handing it to Ian.

'Surprise,' she said, and watched the smile leave his face as his eyes sobered.

'What's this, Shirley?'

'Open it and see.'

Slowly he undid the paper, lifting out the lovely clock. She watched the warm, rich colour flooding his cheeks.

'What — what's this in aid of?'

'It's a 'wee minding,' as the local people call it, with my grateful thanks for all you've done for Grandfather and me.'

'I've done absolutely nothing beyond my job, Shirley!' Ian exclaimed, his face still coloured with embarrassment.

'Don't you like it?' she asked anxiously.

'Like it! Of course I do — anybody would! But that's not the point.'

'It's precisely the point,' she said gaily. 'Put it on your desk, Ian. It will remind you of — of at least two big successes. Would you like me to take surgery tomorrow morning or evening?'

'Morning, please,' Ian said, though he was looking at her rather uncomfortably. How he hated to be thanked, Shirley thought lovingly.

Yet if she had not come to Inverdorran and had never met Ian, just what would her life have become? She shivered a little at the thought, even as he rose to go, the gift held awkwardly in his hand.

'Well, cheerio, Shirley. See you tomorrow. And — thank you very much.'

'Cheerio,' she said gently.

★ ★ ★

The following morning Shirley was a little late for surgery. It had taken longer to attend to her grandfather than usual, and to settle him for a restful and relaxing morning.

He had made no further mention of seeing Brigadier Maxwell attending to his roses, and he was showing signs of returning strength again. Shirley hoped he had forgotten the incident, and was glad to discuss a controversial article in his latest copy of a medical journal, just arrived.

Shirley hurried into a packed surgery, and it was only after she was sitting at the big old desk, and ringing for her first patient, that she realised she didn't have one single qualm as she walked through the door.

She was in complete command of herself, and the job. With a thankful heart, she realised that she was now completely better, and ready to tackle anything in the way of medicine.

Her fourth patient was a young mother with a small girl who looked very sorry for herself, with streaming eyes and nose, and a dry cough.

'She seems to have picked up an awful cold, or something,' the mother said, 'though we haven't done anything unusual.'

'You feel she doesn't deserve it?'

Shirley smiled. 'Er — Mrs Mitchell — and Pamela?'

'That's right. I've got two older girls as well, and I do try to make sure they change out of wet things.'

'Mmm.' Shirley was examining the child, who stood in front of her patiently, even though she looked sickly and heavy eyed.

'No signs of a rash?' she asked Mrs Mitchell.

'A rash? No.'

'Has she had measles?'

The young woman hesitated, shaking her head.

'No, you never hear of the wee ones having measles hereabouts these days, not for a long while, anyway.'

'No, they all have their inoculations. I suppose Pamela and the other girls have all been done?'

'There seemed to be no need,' Mrs Mitchell said quickly. 'You don't think it's measles, Doctor?'

Shirley didn't reply for a moment.

'I think you ought to pop her into

bed. I'll give you something for her now, and I'll be along to examine her properly later. I think it will have to be tomorrow.'

She made a note to ask Ian about the small boy he had seen in Camusling. They didn't want a measles epidemic on their hands!

Her next patient had brought a passport photograph to be signed, and Shirley smiled at the unflattering likeness to the young student who was going to France on a working holiday, and who had expected to see Ian.

'My mother says I'll be liable to get arrested with a face like that,' he said, grinning.

'I'm sure Dr Andrews will appreciate it,' Shirley told him, her eyes full of laughter. 'It's an excellent likeness.' He departed with good wishes from her, and the old gentleman who came in to the next ring of her bell had difficulty in breathing.

Gently Shirley invited him to sit down, and got back to work.

It was almost lunch-time when Shirley saw the last of her patients, and she sat for a moment writing up notes before going round to the kitchen for a quick lunch. She must try to get hold of Ian as soon as possible, and find out if anything further had developed with that child in Camusling.

Mrs Ross was just putting down the telephone when she walked in.

'Oh, Miss Shirley, that was Jock Sinclair. You know Jock at the garage?'

'Of course I do.' Shirley smiled warmly.

He and Mrs Sinclair had been two of the first five people she had met when she came to Inverdorran . . . apart from Neil, she remembered, and she always thought of the Sinclairs with special affection. They had given her help just when she needed it.

'Mrs Sinclair isn't a bit well,' Mrs Ross went on. 'She's taken to her bed. Would you manage to go along and see her after you've had a bite to eat?'

'Of course I will,' Shirley agreed. 'Is lunch ready now?'

'Yes. Your grandfather has already had his, and has eaten every bite. That's a change, I must say — much more like his old self. I'll put the soup out now.'

'Fine. I'll be through in a moment, Mrs Ross. I must just telephone Dr Andrews first of all.'

Mrs Ross turned away, shaking her head. The girl was just like her grandfather when he was busy. The number of bowls of cold soup she'd had to throw out in her time!

But there was no reply from Ian's number, and Shirley made a note to ring him after she had been to see Mrs Sinclair.

She got out her grandfather's old bone-shaker some thirty minutes later, and drove out to the garage on the outskirts of Inverdorran. How strange the place had seemed when she first saw it, and how familiar it all looked now!

★ ★ ★

Jock Sinclair was delighted to see her, but he was obviously anxious about his wife, so they talked only briefly before she went to examine her patient.

'She's upstairs lying down,' he said, leading the way. 'She feels very hot and her eyes seem a bit sore, though it appears to be more of a wee cough that's troubling her.'

He rambled on a little, but already Shirley was hurrying towards the bed, where Mrs Sinclair lay restless and feverish looking.

This time she was able to examine her patient thoroughly, and this time there was no mistake. Mrs Sinclair had a fine dose of measles.

'Have you had measles before?' she asked.

The older woman shook her head.

'No, I was the lucky one when I was a youngster.'

Perhaps not so lucky, thought Shirley,

knowing that measles could be even more distressing in an adult.

'Do you know young Mrs Mitchell and her wee girls?' Shirley asked, remembering the young woman who had called in at the surgery that morning. 'The youngest one is called Pamela.'

'Mrs Mitchell is my niece,' Mrs Sinclair said. 'She leaves wee Pamela here with me when she goes to Inverness.'

Shirley nodded, her eyes sober. She was pretty sure she would find the rash out on Pamela Mitchell when she called to examine her later.

'You'll need careful nursing, Mrs Sinclair,' she said, and went downstairs to make arrangements with Jock.

'She'll have everything she needs,' he declared. 'Whatever you think best, Doctor. Geoffrey Lewis and I will manage. You know our young schoolmaster, don't you? He's our boarder.'

Shirley's eyes grew cool. 'Yes, I know him,' she said.

Jock looked at her intently.

'Has he been upsetting you, Doctor? He's inclined to get carried away with his enthusiasms.'

'Yes, he is,' she agreed briefly, and Jock Sinclair was in no doubt that his boarder had displeased young Dr Baxter.

'I must go and make some phone calls,' she said, smiling a little ruefully. 'Don't worry about Mrs Sinclair. We'll soon have her on her feet again.'

But there was a look of anxiety on Shirley's face as she drove home, then hurried to the telephone, and dialled Ian's home number.

Getting no reply, she put down the phone, then picked it up again and re-dialled.

She was about to hang up when the receiver at the other end was lifted, and a clear, lilting, but slightly breathless, voice answered.

'Dr Andrews' residence. Can I take a message?'

Shirley paused, taken aback.

'Er . . . may I speak to Dr Andrews, please?'

Mrs White must have someone visiting her today, she mused.

'I'm sorry, he has just been called out,' the girl told her, 'but I can put a message on his pad, if you'll just tell me . . . '

'Who's speaking, please?' Shirley interrupted.

'I'm Alison Grant,' the girl told her. 'I'm Dr Andrews' fiancée.'

A Little White Lie

Shirley was hardly conscious of putting down the phone. She could still hear the faint, sweet voice of the girl asking who was speaking, but she was powerless to reply. Ian's fiancée! Why had no-one ever mentioned that he was going to be married?

Numbed, Shirley sat, trying desperately to remember some incident, some sentence or word even, that would have warned her Ian was not free. She just couldn't believe it. Surely it couldn't be true.

Shirley sat for a long time, trying to clear her thoughts. She had not found out because she had taken it for granted that Ian was single and unattached. In all the times they had spent together, they had talked mainly of medical matters, of her grandfather's health, her own problems when she had lost her

144

confidence so badly, and other small things which worried her at the time.

It was Ian's gentle, but firm, support which had helped her to stand on her feet again, and she had got used to talking about herself, not about him. He had been so overburdened with work and so tired many a time when he sat down to relax with her, that he probably had not the energy to talk of his own personal matters, and no doubt assumed she knew all about Alison Grant.

She remembered other occasions when she'd had to ask a name, or the location of a small village which he had assumed she must know, and even a relationship between one patient and another.

'I forget you haven't lived here all your life, Shirley,' he had told her, grinning, and she had taken it as a compliment.

But even as these thoughts chased one another round and round in her mind, there were others crowding in, even more disquieting. She remembered Ian's embarrassment when she gave him the gift of the desk clock, how he had tried to say something, then let it go.

There had been other similar occasions when he had eyed her a little bit tentatively, no doubt wondering if she knew he was not free, yet hesitating to cause her any embarrassment, either because she did not know . . . or, even worse, if she did!

* * *

It seemed hours to Shirley before she finally managed to pull herself together, then slowly she made her way upstairs to her grandfather's room. The old man was reading a novel by Sir Walter Scott.

'Always promised myself I'd get through 'Ivanhoe' beyond the first dozen or so pages, one day,' he said. 'I'd just be getting into it at night, when some inconsiderate baby would decide to arrive, and cause me to throw the book aside. Now I can enjoy it in peace.'

When she did not reply, he laid it aside, removed his reading glasses and put on his normal pair.

'Gracious, Shirley, what's happened? Is it some patient or other? Something serious?'

She shook her head, but the sympathy and concern in her grandfather's voice was too much, and soon Shirley was sobbing her heart out in his arms.

'Oh, Grandfather, I hardly know how to explain. You see, it's Ian. I — I didn't know about Miss . . . about Alison Grant, and I . . . '

Dr Baxter bit his lip, feeling chagrined as he stroked her hair. It was all his fault. Once or twice he had suspected Shirley was beginning to have special feelings for Ian Andrews, yet he had hesitated over dropping her a hint. If he had mentioned Miss Grant early on, she might not be having this heartache.

Why hadn't Ian himself told her, he

thought angrily. Yet maybe Ian had just felt as he did, that they were presuming to know Shirley's feelings, when they could have been quite wrong. She had other men friends besides Ian.

'Have a good weep, lassie,' her grandfather said, finding her a hankie. 'I should maybe have dropped you the hint, but I didn't know how you felt about Ian . . .'

'But you suspected, Grandfather?' Shirley asked tearfully.

He was about to agree, when he paused for thought. Maybe a little white lie was in order. He knew so well what a blow her pride must have suffered, since her feelings were so parallel to his own.

'That I didn't,' he declared stoutly. 'If I had suspected even the tiniest wee bit, I'd have seen to it that you knew about Miss Grant. I'd have warned you off, never fear. But you never gave yourself away, not once.'

'Didn't I?' Shirley gazed at him hopefully. If her grandfather had not suspected, then maybe she hadn't worn her heart on her sleeve for Ian to see, either.

Her heart ached, and she knew that she would have a deep, inward struggle before she could put her feelings behind her, and carry on as though nothing had happened. But it would help quite a lot if she did not have to feel humiliated in front of Ian Andrews.

She sat up and smoothed back her hair.

'I'm sorry, Grandfather.' She managed to smile. 'I shouldn't be putting my troubles on to you.'

'Then who else would you come to?' he asked.

'I was ringing Ian up because I think there may be a few cases of measles brewing up, and I wanted to know how to go about certain things.'

Old Dr Baxter looked at the time.

'Well, I think you ought to forget all about it tonight. If there's any urgency, we'll know soon enough. All the patients know where we live. I prescribe for my granddaughter a bite of supper up here with me, on a tray, then a nice warm bath and early to bed.

'By morning you won't have to depend on Ian's advice so much regarding my patients and their measles, because I'm going to tell you what to do. You can ask him about his own cases, of course. I wish I'd a penny, though, for every case of measles I've put through my hands!'

'But . . .'

'But nothing. Haven't you noticed it's just laziness which is keeping me in bed these days? I'm as fit as a fiddle. I was only stopping here to get through 'Ivanhoe' and one or two others, but I think I'll still be reading them when I'm ninety!'

'Now off you go, my dear, and try not to worry too much. I know it'll hurt a lot, but it gives you a chance to show what you're made of. And that's good stock! I used to tell that to Colin, your father . . .'

Shirley nodded, and went downstairs to fetch the supper tray. She felt tired and bruised, but she knew her grandfather was right. It would be a painful struggle, but in the end, she'd get over it.

Even as she carried the tray upstairs, she was aware of a new maturity. She felt as though her girlhood was behind her.

Old Dr Baxter was as good as his word, and next morning he was up, dressed and downstairs ten minutes ahead of Shirley, who looked pale and heavy eyed, but quite composed when she arrived downstairs. She, too, was concerned to see her grandfather sitting at the table, then a great deal comforted by his presence.

'You must promise me to have a rest in the afternoon,' she said, 'and to break yourself in by staying up longer periods each day. For today, you're only up till lunch-time.'

'I've been doing that for years,' he told her. 'It used to be the only way I could turn one day into two! Oh, all right, Dr Shirley, I promise.'

They grinned at one another.

* ★ *

'Now tell me all about this measles outbreak, and I'll tell you the best way to deal with it, here at Inverdorran. All these things are bound to be strange to a young lass trained in London with all its rules and regulations. Sometimes they strangle us with them, so that we can't do our work. What's that letter you've got there in the post?'

Shirley opened the official-looking letter.

'It's the inquiry into Walter Maguire's accident. It's to be held next Wednesday in the school.'

She turned a pale face to the old man, who was attacking his porridge with enjoyment.

'Well, one thing at a time. We'll worry about that next Tuesday night, or even Wednesday morning. After you've finished breakfast, ring Ian about the measles.'

He gave her a direct look, and Shirley flushed, then met his eyes squarely.

'Certainly. We have to compare notes.' She smiled. 'It's all right, Grandfather, I can handle it. Ian won't even guess.'

'That's my girl.'

'I'll ask him to bring his — his fiancée over for supper this evening, shall I? I'd rather like to meet her, and I — I'd prefer it to be here than somewhere else.'

'You do that. In fact, if I have a good long rest all afternoon, I don't see why I can't stagger down to join you. Will that help?'

She forced back the tears, and kissed him.

'Oh, Grandfather! Whatever would I have done without you?'

'You've got another letter, I see,' her grandfather said, but this time she merely smiled and slipped it into her cardigan pocket. It was the usual weekly newsy one from Brian Wills.

She would read it later.

That evening, Shirley looked gay and pretty in a flowered jersey dress in

153

shades of blue, and her chestnut hair had been brushed till it shone. She welcomed her guests graciously with a smile which showed nothing of her hurt and pain inside.

Alison Grant was a small, slender girl with bell-shaped fair hair. Shirley felt tall and well built beside her. She greeted the girl warmly, then drew breath as she turned to Ian. For a small second the pain was in her eyes, but she smiled cheerfully, and welcomed him with a light laugh.

'We won't have to talk shop tonight, Ian, will we? For once we had better allow the patients to rest peacefully in their beds without their ears ringing.'

'Quite right, Dr Baxter.' Alison laughed.

'Oh, please just call me Shirley. Dr Baxter is my grandfather!'

'And I'm Alison. I've met your grandfather already, you know . . .'

Ian watched the two girls walk ahead of him into the lounge, and he paused for a moment to remove his coat, his eyes sober. He felt he had been a bit

154

unperceptive of Shirley, though once or twice he had pondered for a moment, wondering if the warmth of friendship she showed him did not contain something more.

When she gave him the desk clock, he had felt rather uneasy, and now, for one revealing moment, he had caught the flash of pain in her eyes.

Ian bit his lip as he went to join the others. He wished now he'd had a bit of foresight, and had brought Alison into the conversation when they had first met. Yet there never seemed to be time for talking about personal matters, and Shirley's troubles had always seemed paramount.

'Yes, I live in Edinburgh,' Alison was saying. 'I keep house for my father, who is a solicitor. I used to think I would like to have been a nurse, or something . . . '

'Better not.' Shirley laughed. 'If you're going to marry Ian, one person involved in medicine in a family is quite enough. I don't think Grandfather and

I find more than one topic of conversation each evening, beyond the events of the day.'

'Oh, I expect it will be the same with Ian and me,' said Alison, looking shyly at him. 'I'll let him do the talking while I listen!'

'Ian's a very fortunate fellow,' said Dr Baxter. 'A good, sympathetic ear is an asset to anyone.'

'It certainly is,' Shirley said. 'As a matter of fact, Ian has helped me in the past, just by listening. I — I was very grateful.'

She turned to look at him, and he flushed, then smiled.

It would have to be a fine man who deserved her, thought Ian Andrews, looking at the proud tilt of her head, her beauty and charm.

Then his eyes were on Alison, his sweetheart since they were in their teens. She had brought news that her father was planning to re-marry, a charming, sensible woman whom he had known for some years.

This would make quite a difference to their own plans, and he and Alison were already talking over wedding arrangements.

'Before I forget,' he said, 'that sick child, the Mitchell baby, had eaten a sour apple . . . '

He broke off as they all started to laugh.

'It's time I served up the supper,' said Shirley, and hurried towards the kitchen. It was odd, but she felt much better than she had expected, and if she did not think too deeply, she could keep herself quite cheery.

She liked Alison Grant very much, and she could see how Ian obviously preferred a small, quiet girl. Perhaps they would never have suited, thought Shirley sadly.

Sighing, she began to wheel the supper trolley towards the lounge.

★ ★ ★

Next morning, Shirley caught a whiff of rose perfume as she walked out of the back door, and it brought Brigadier

Maxwell to mind. She had not seen him for several days, but that was not unusual.

Had her grandfather seen him while he was walking about downstairs, and had they perhaps had a row while she was out on her rounds?

Shirley hurried indoors for a word with Mrs Ross.

'I was wondering if Grandfather had spotted him, and they'd had words,' she said, as she explained. 'I'd feel very annoyed if he had been so ungrateful.'

'Don't worry yourself. I'd soon get to know,' said Mrs Ross. 'However, I wouldn't put it past the doctor, or the Brigadier, for that matter. Dear knows what gets into them over a lovely flower like a rose. They both love the blooms, but use the prickles to jag one another!'

Shirley laughed heartily, though her eyes sobered again. She thought she had better go and see Brigadier Maxwell to find out what the matter was. She recognised one or two items belonging to him in her grandfather's gardening shed. If he did not want to come again, those would have to be returned.

This time when she rang the bell at Ardlui, she only had to wait a moment before Catriona Maxwell threw open the door.

'Oh, it's you, Shirley,' she said, and her disappointment was obvious. Intuitively Shirley knew that she had been expecting Neil Fraser.

'I really came to see the Brigadier,' she said. 'Is he at home at the moment?'

'Come in. As a matter of fact, I've been thinking I ought to send for you, but Father isn't very amenable when it comes to his health.'

'Then he isn't well?' asked Shirley anxiously.

'He has rheumatism — had it for years. But sometimes it seems to flare up on him. Through here, Shirley.'

Catriona led the way into the lounge,

where the Brigadier was sitting by the fireside, a blanket round his knees.

'Oh dear,' said Shirley. 'I didn't know you were troubled with rheumatism. You should have sent for me, Brigadier!'

'And what could you do,' he asked, 'beyond giving me some sort of pill which does no good at all?'

'Some rheumatisms can be treated more easily than others.'

'Well *my* sort doesn't just vanish with the first pill,' the Brigadier said, almost proudly. 'Heat — that's the answer. A good hot water bottle, and a rub up. That's the stuff. That'll soon get rid of it.'

'How long have you had this bout?'

'That's the devil of it,' the Brigadier admitted. 'Too long! It should have gone by now with all these hot water bottles. Can you really do something for me, young lady?'

Shirley grinned. 'I'll have a jolly good try.'

She wrote out a prescription and

handed it to Catriona, who said she would lose no time in having it made up, and would see that her father stuck to it.

★ ★ ★

'I'll give it a try,' he said, grudgingly, 'but only because the show will soon be here.'

'What show?' Shirley asked.

'The Flower Show, of course!' Brigadier Maxwell began to doubt her competence all over again. How could anyone forget the Flower Show?

'I've got one or two beauties just coming into bloom. I'll get them there, if Catriona has to push me in a wheelchair! Oh, and I intend to put in that pure white your grandfather has grown . . . that 'Shirley Baxter'! Is it named after you?'

'My grandmother, really,' said Shirley, 'though perhaps I can share it a little.'

'Well,' his voice grew gruff, 'it's not at

161

all bad. Seems a shame not to show it, you know.'

Shirley was looking at him doubtfully.

'I'm not sure whether Grandfather would want it to be shown,' she said hesitantly.

'Not show it! Of course he would show it if he could. Only he's not quite up to it, is he, so I'll do it for him. But you'd better keep quiet about it, Shirley. Your grandfather is not a reasonable man over roses. Promise me you'll say nothing.'

Shirley stared at him uneasily. She wasn't at all happy about secrecy of this kind, especially when she remembered how her grandfather had reacted to seeing his rival among his roses. Yet something like this might help the Brigadier to throw off this crippling bout of rheumatism. She was convinced her treatment would help, and the Flower Show coming up would spur him into following her advice!

'Very well,' she said. 'I promise.'

'Good girl,' the Brigadier said, well

pleased. 'I'll let you know if your pills are any good!'

★　★　★

Catriona came with her to the door, thanking her for helping her father.

'He gets crotchety when he's in pain,' she said. 'In fact, I've asked . . . ' She stopped, looking a bit embarrassed.

'Asked what?'

'Oh, nothing really. Er — have you seen Neil recently?' Her voice was deliberately casual.

'Not for a day or two. I'm tending to get busier now that I know the practice, and people know me.'

Catriona nodded. 'I can imagine. I envy you quite a lot your career, and I know Neil admires your skill as a doctor.'

Shirley said nothing.

Catriona always seemed to want to probe her relationship with Neil Fraser.

'He can be awfully stubborn and unreasonable, you know,' Catriona went on, and Shirley nodded, remembering Neil's anger when he thought her evidence might be slanted against him at the inquiry over Maguire's accident.

'I wanted us to go into partnership in Beauty and Fashion, in Edinburgh, when — when we got married . . . Beauty for women, and grooming for men, but he was so full of this awful sports complex. We — we quarrelled over it, and I broke off our engagement. I've always known, though, that he would see things differently when he had time to consider.

'The complex has just been like a fever with him, and he's been so unreasonable over everything else. We couldn't even discuss it. But now things could easily be different.'

'Different?' Shirley asked.

'Yes — over Walter Maguire and that accident. I mean, if Neil loses — well — he might come to his senses, and give up the idea once and for all. Edinburgh would be so much better for us, so much more civilised.'

'And you'd like that? For Neil to give up this project which means so much to him?' She looked at Catriona, thinking again how attractive she was. Yet underneath that serene beauty, Shirley felt there was a hard core of selfishness.

Catriona might even have come to accept the sports complex if she had not been so determined to have things her own way. Would a girl like this be right for Neil, Shirley wondered uneasily.

She thought about the eager light in his eyes, and his quick decisive voice as he showed her round the sports complex, and something stirred in her. Again she could only define it as a sense of uneasiness for Neil. She would hate it if he lost this project, and be disillusioned after all the work he had done.

'It would be much the best thing for him, Shirley,' Catriona was saying. 'Isn't the inquiry on Wednesday?'

She could not be trying to influence me, could she, pondered Shirley, and decided to leave before any further discussion.

'That's right — on Wednesday,' she said briskly. 'I'll look in again to see your father, and in the meantime, don't hesitate to send for me if you are anxious.'

The door closed behind her, and Shirley walked briskly up the lane, deep in thought. What was Catriona Maxwell thinking about? Did her own selfishness blind her to unhappiness in others? If Catriona really loved Neil, wouldn't she be behind him, fighting on his side all the way? Her thoughts were so full of him, she almost jumped as she rounded a corner and met him, no doubt making for Ardlui.

'Why, hello, Neil, I've been hoping to see you,' Shirley said, smiling.

There was no response in the dark-rimmed eyes which stared into her own. He was thinner, she decided, running a professional eye over him. The dark shadows suggested that he had been sleeping badly.

'I've been busy,' he said briefly.

'Yes, I know. But, Neil, I do think you ought to take it easy. I mean — nothing is more important than . . . '

She was about to talk about his health, but he turned away abruptly.

'I know what is important to me, Shirley. I'm just disappointed that I haven't been able to show you *how* important it is. Now if you'll excuse me, Catriona says her father is off colour with his rheumatism and could use a bit of company.'

She hesitated, wondering what to say to put things right between them, but even as she stood looking at him silently, Neil turned away and walked towards Ardlui, the Maxwell home.

She watched him go, then walked towards Beech House feeling sick at heart.

★ ★ ★

The telephone was ringing when she arrived home, and Shirley could hear

Mrs Ross muttering as she hurried to answer it. Her grandfather was not at his usual place by the fireside, and Shirley knew he must have gone up to bed. He was keeping his promise to the letter.

'It's all right, I'll answer it, Mrs Ross,' she called, running to pick up the receiver. It was Ian.

'Oh, thank goodness I've found you, Shirley,' he said. 'I'm at Camusling. I've got four more confirmed cases among the children, and when I telephoned home, Alison said Jock Sinclair had rung up . . .'

'Jock Sinclair! Then . . .'

'Jock Sinclair has been ringing for you, Miss Shirley,' Mrs Ross broke in. 'I told him you would not be long. He sounded very worried.'

'Thank you, Mrs Ross,' she said, then spoke again to Ian. 'He's been on for me here, as well. If you see to the children, Ian, I'll go long and attend to Mrs Sinclair.'

The older woman was very sick, her

temperature as high as Shirley cared to see it.

'I'll have to get her temperature down,' she said to Jock. 'I'll give her an injection, and I'd better sponge her down. She's very hot.'

'She's been delirious, Dr Shirley,' Jock said, his kindly face grave with worry. 'She's been shouting out all sorts of rubbish, and seeing things that aren't there.'

'Don't worry, Jock, she's over the worst, I'm sure. I'll need some more boiled water, cooled down, Jock,' she said as a figure came into the room.

'He's getting it for you, Shirley,' Geoffrey Lewis said, and Shirley turned round, her eyes growing cool.

She'd forgotten he was the Sinclairs' boarder.

'Is she very ill? I — I was just wondering . . . '

'Could you please find something to do elsewhere, Mr Lewis?' Shirley said, unable to keep the irritation from her voice.

Suddenly, Jock slipped into the room with a fresh basin of water. Putting it down quietly, he nodded at Shirley, whose sleeves were rolled up as she attended to Mrs Sinclair.

Quietly, he gripped Geoffrey's arm.

'Come on, Mr Lewis,' he said firmly. 'I think you and I ought to have a quiet word together.'

No Decision

Here's a cup of tea for you, Doctor.'

Shirley Baxter rose, her bones aching with cramp, and turned to thank white-faced Jock Sinclair as he came into the bedroom.

'How is she?'

For a moment, Shirley did not answer. Mrs Sinclair had reacted badly to her attack of measles, but now Shirley felt that her temperature was dropping, and she was beginning to respond to the drugs she had been given.

'Better, I think, Jock,' she said.

Her fingers were on Mrs Sinclair's pulse, then she sat back and drank her tea gratefully, while Jock sat down beside her. Janet's illness had obviously shaken him.

'You should try to get some sleep, Jock,' she said kindly, seeing the tired lines round his eyes.

'There will be plenty of time for sleep when Janet is sitting up and giving me a lecture for not changing my socks,' Jock said. 'She's always so bright and busy about the house. I — I'm not used to having it quiet, like this.'

'Well, I think I can promise you that you'll be catching it again in a week or two.' Shirley smiled. 'She's having a refreshing sleep now and her temperature is down, too, so I wouldn't be surprised if she tried to get out of bed in a few more days. I'll see to it that she takes a proper rest, though, after a bout like this, Jock. Don't you worry.'

'I'm not — not any more — with you to look after her. I — I honestly don't know what to say to you, to thank you for looking after Janet like this.' Jock's face had gone red as he felt he could not adequately express his gratitude. It was like coming out into the sunshine to see Janet looking even a little bit more like herself.

'Say no more, Jock,' Shirley told him.

'I'm only doing my job. Now, have you anyone else to help you? Besides Geoffrey Lewis, I mean?'

'Mrs Clark comes in, and as for young Mr Lewis, there's no need to worry about him. He's a nice enough young man and a good teacher, but he's an awful fanatic over some things and doesn't mind who he roasts till he gets his own way. He's all out for preservation, and to prevent things changing, but the world keeps changing all the time.

'We've just got to go along with it, and do our best not to allow those changes to spoil what we've got already. He and I have had a long talk, Dr Shirley, and I don't think he'll be bothering you for a while.'

Shirley sighed. She was beginning to be aware of her own fatigue, as she stood up and collected her bag.

'Now it's my turn to thank you,' she said, with a smile. 'I agree that Geoffrey is a nice man and a fine teacher, but he can make himself a nuisance at times.

Let me know if you're worried at all, Jock, and see that you give these tablets to Mrs Sinclair by the clock.'

'OK, and thanks, Doctor.'

Shirley made her way home and climbed into bed. It had never felt more comfortable. She thought a little about Geoffrey Lewis, then her thoughts went on to Neil Fraser and his strained, unhappy face, last time she had seen him. If only I could help him, Shirley thought. Somehow she felt it would be a great loss all round if Neil was forced to abandon his project, after all he had done.

She had come to think of him as a man of courage who could fight for his ideals. Somehow she wanted Neil to stay that way.

★ ★ ★

Shirley was down to breakfast the following morning rather later than usual, and her grandfather had already finished his porridge and eggs, and had

174

started on his toast and marmalade.

'You were late last night.'

'It was Janet Sinclair,' she said. 'She reacted badly to the measles, but she's over the worst now. I'll just have toast and coffee, Mrs Ross. I'm not very hungry.'

'You'll have an egg, too,' her grandfather said. 'You're using up too much energy to go starving yourself, so eat up.'

Shirley said nothing but carried on with her breakfast. After they finished, as they sat in the lounge, old Dr Baxter eyed her shrewdly.

'Ian Andrews phoned,' he said quietly.

He saw her mouth tightening, and sighed inwardly. Ian's latest news would probably be another small hurt, but Shirley had better hear it from him.

'The date of the wedding has been fixed. It's a month on Saturday.'

'Oh . . . fine,' Shirley said rather tonelessly. Her heart was still sore over Ian. One could not turn one's feelings on and off like a tap.

'We're both invited to Edinburgh for the celebrations, and he's arranging for somebody to take over in case of emergencies.'

'I see.' She glanced at the pile of mail, and she saw a letter from Brian Wills on top. To distract her grandfather's attention, she opened the letter, reading the hastily-scrawled lines.

'Well!' she said, reading on. 'Well, this is interesting.'

'What?'

'Brian Wills — you know, Dr Wills who worked with me in London — is hoping to be travelling in this area next week. He says he would like to call if he may . . .'

She was reading on. Brian said he had something important he wished to discuss with her.

'He can stay here, if he likes,' her grandfather suggested.

The prospect of another young doctor calling on Shirley pleased the old man. Surely he would get her mind away from Ian Andrews at least! It would do her good to have this young man's companionship for a few days.

Shirley smiled with sudden pleasure. It would be lovely to see Brian again, and to hear all the news of the hospital. For a while she had been rather unhappy there, when she lost her confidence and was so afraid that the career she loved would be over, almost before it had begun.

In those days Brian had been a good friend who had helped and encouraged her. But now she could think of that part of her life with great pleasure, her confidence restored, and that was all thanks to Ian.

Old Dr Baxter watched the shadows on her expressive face, and decided it was time she was brought out of herself. Shirley was far too inclined to take things to heart.

'I'm coming out with you on your rounds today,' Dr Baxter said decisively.

'Grandfather! Indeed you are not! Being up on your feet and walking about is one thing, but travelling around is another.'

'Do you think I've just been staggering from one chair to another while you've been out? If so, you'll have to think again. I got my sea-legs back with going for walks. I suppose you're thinking you've nabbed all my practice, young woman?'

'Oh no!' Shirley said, taken aback, though she caught sight of a gleam in his eyes. 'Not at all, Grandfather . . . '

'Well, I've got to start back some time. You just carry on as usual. I'll come and watch, and just see how you're shaping up as a doctor.'

'Yes, Grandfather,' Shirley said, rather dolefully. Her ways might not be his, and maybe there would be storm clouds ahead because of that!

★ ★ ★

On Saturday, old Dr Baxter had an extra five minutes in bed. Fortunately Shirley's cases had mainly been those

178

patients who were now recovering from measles, and a few with small injuries. They had even called on old Mr Elliott, who was now in fine fettle. When they finally returned, her grandfather was glad to rest for a little longer than usual.

'Brigadier Maxwell's at the back door, Miss Shirley,' whispered Mrs Ross, out of old Dr Baxter's earshot. 'He's cutting off some of the doctor's roses, and putting them in a long box.'

'Oh dear,' Shirley said, hurrying outside.

The Brigadier looked to be full of beans, as he turned to greet Shirley with a smile. It was a splendid morning, the sun already warm on their faces, and the air clear and pure.

'How is the rheumatism?' she asked.

'Ah well — I must admit that your tablets did the trick, Dr Shirley. They worked better than heat — in this instance, at least. I'm not a taker of pills, you know. They might mend one thing, then go on to injure another.'

Shirley hid a smile. The Brigadier would not go down without a fight!

'And now you feel better?'

'Fit enough for the Flower Show,' he agreed. 'Isn't it a splendid morning? Hamish Baxter would have been in good form if he had been well enough.'

'Oh, but . . . ' Shirley was about to say that her grandfather was now a great deal better, but she thought better of it.

She only hoped that Brigadier Maxwell would help himself to the roses, then take himself off before her grandfather appeared, looking for his breakfast!

He was snipping them with a great deal of care. He looked at each bloom lovingly.

'There, then. The 'Shirley Baxter,'' he said it almost reverently, then seemed to collect himself.

'Quite a nice little rose,' he said briskly. 'Deserves to have an outing to the Flower Show. Well, Miss Shirley, I'll be away. I'll — ah, let you know how we get on, shall I, 'Shirley Baxter' and I? 'Morning, my dear.'

Shirley watched him go, then turned to go back indoors. A moment later her grandfather appeared at the back door, then slowly he walked towards his rose garden. After a moment's hesitation, she followed along behind him.

It was a new step in his recovery, thought Shirley. Old Dr Baxter had pulled himself round from a serious illness, first of all by sitting up in bed, then walking slowly round the house. Going for walks and sitting in with her to greet his patients had been a milestone, but the real testing time, when he was once more among his beloved roses, had now come.

This was something he had not felt able to face, until now. This was something which really touched his heart.

Without a word, he walked about, examining each bush carefully, seeing how lovingly they had been treated, the leaves shining, dead flowers snipped off, and the new blooms growing with such perfection. He bent down and allowed the soil to trickle through his fingers. Here and there he saw the odd weed which had been overlooked, and these were removed in a twinkling.

Shirley hardly dared to breathe, but at length the old man turned, and she could see the suspicion of a tear in his eyes. He cleared his throat, and she braced herself to answer a barrage of questions, but none came. Instead he walked slowly back indoors without a word.

'Where's my breakfast, Mrs Ross?' he demanded. 'I'd enjoy it very much, thank you.'

With a smile, Mrs Ross put his porridge before him.

Shirley sat down and poured herself a cup of coffee.

'I'm only on emergency calls today,' she said. 'I'm keeping my fingers crossed that there are none.'

'Why? What are you doing today?'

'Buying a new suit for Ian's wedding,' she said, and he knew this was her last word on the subject of Ian Andrews.

'Get blue,' he said. 'Your grandmother always looked lovely in blue — the colour of periwinkles.'

'All right, I'll try for blue,' she said lightly.

In fact, it was a soft blue like a bluebell seen through the mist, but it suited Shirley to perfection, as she tried it on for her grandfather's benefit later that evening.

'Is Nancy as bonnie as you?' he asked suddenly. 'Let's see, she's — how old?'

'Sixteen — almost seventeen, in fact, and Paul is now twenty. I sent him a present last week. Nancy is the real beauty, if you want to know. She takes after Mother.'

'Hmm. I've a fancy to see them,' Dr Baxter said musingly. 'It made me think, lying up there, about how much we miss by not going the extra mile. I'll give myself another week or two to get my strength back, then we'll have to think how a reunion could be accomplished. It's time I got to know my family properly.'

'Oh, Grandfather, that would be wonderful! I know Mother would love it.'

'And how about your father?'

'So would he. I know he would!'

'Don't ever quarrel with your own kith and kin, lass. As you get older, you realise that people are more important than possessions, and time is better than money . . . Och, who's that now?'

Shirley hid a smile as he broke off his little homily when the bell shrilled.

'It must be one of your important people,' she said, and went to the door.

* * *

It was Brigadier Maxwell who did not wait for an invitation, but came striding in, his eyes lit up with excitement, the rich colour in his face. There was a carrier bag under his arm.

'What a day!' he exclaimed. 'What a show! Where's Baxter? I've got something here to show him which will get him on his feet again. It's high time he was back in harness.'

'What's that? So it's yourself, Maxwell! What have you been up to now?' asked the doctor, appearing behind Shirley.

Firmly she led the way into the sitting-room, and made both men sit down.

'You can talk about your roses more comfortably from an armchair,' she said. 'I'll get a pot of tea.'

'Not till you've seen this,' said the Brigadier, lifting out a beautiful silver cup.

Dr Baxter stared at it. 'So you've made it this year,' he said. 'Though if I'd been fit . . . '

The Brigadier interrupted his tirade.

'You would have shown your 'Shirley Baxter.' I know. Well, I showed her for you. Mind you, my own Pink Sunset gave it a run for the money. It was a close thing — a very close thing. By next year, my Pink Sunset will walk away with it, very likely, but this year it's yours, Baxter. So here you are.'

He handed the old doctor the lovely silver cup, and Shirley saw her grandfather bite his lip, his hands trembling, as he held it.

'So it won — my 'Shirley Baxter' won,' he said, awed, and for a while both men sat without speaking. It was a precious moment for both of them, Shirley realised.

'Well, that's all right then,' the Brigadier said. 'I knew you'd do it this time, Baxter.'

'No, I didn't. You did it for me,' said Dr Baxter gruffly. 'In fact, you'll have been neglecting your Pink Sunset for me, no doubt. I like to win, but I like a fair fight, Maxwell, and this has not been one. You've been putting your back into doing my stock at the expense of your own.'

'I never have . . . '

'Don't argue. I've seen you at it, and no-one can tell me that any person, other than yourself, has been in among my bushes. Well, I don't call that a fair fight . . . '

'Now you're just being stupid, as usual . . . '

Shirley smiled, and went to make the tea. She excused herself after pouring theirs. She would leave them to enjoy one another's company.

★   ★   ★

The following Wednesday, Shirley drove into Inverness to attend the tribunal which was to decide who was to blame for Walter Maguire's accident, and if any compensation had to be paid.

Her thoughts were again full of Neil, and she could imagine the tension he would be experiencing.

He had seemed to avoid her these days, and for a moment it crossed her mind to wonder whether he was avoiding her as a person, or as a doctor.

He must know he was not glowing with perfect health, as he had been. He had lost weight, and looked as though he was sleeping badly. He was bound to be a very worried man.

Although very nervous, Shirley found the tribunal much less formal than she had anticipated. A committee had been appointed to decide on the case, and the chairman seemed to be a kindly, fair-minded man.

Walter Maguire now walked with the aid of a stick, and Shirley shrewdly suspected that the stick would not be needed much longer after the tribunal. She also caught a glimpse of Geoffrey Lewis and Catriona Maxwell, both deeply interested in the outcome, but for completely different motives.

Geoffrey looked quiet and subdued, however, and Shirley relaxed. He did not look as though he would be much of a threat to Neil.

She watched the young solicitor, who was clerk to the tribunal, going about his affairs with calm efficiency. How rational it all seems, thought Shirley. Then she turned to look at Neil, and was shocked at how haggard he looked.

She had a swift, mental vision of the young man she had met when she first came to Inverdorran, after that long car journey. He had helped her then, and she had thought how purposeful and competent he looked.

Now it seemed to her that Neil was hanging on through grim determination, and if this decision went against him, and he had to pay out a large sum in compensation, then his health would be very seriously affected.

Quietly she listened while an expert on industrial matters described the site of the sports complex, and pointed out the weakness in the area which was being demolished. A great deal of it went over Shirley's head when they went into technical matters, and maps and photographs were closely examined, together with architects' plans.

Witnesses came and went and then it was Neil, stating firmly that safety regulations had been strictly laid down, and he had tried to ensure that the men kept to these regulations. His only hesitation came when he admitted that Walter Maguire had already ignored some of these rules and had to be reprimanded.

'Perhaps it was wrong of me not to dismiss him, but . . . ' Neil glanced towards Mrs Maguire and her eldest son ' . . . he had a family to support, and I decided to give him another chance.'

Shirley could see a muscle twitching nervously. This was what Neil was afraid of. He had prided himself on being a good boss and fair with his men, but he had weakened on one occasion, using his heart instead of his head, and now this had happened, perhaps even as a direct result.

Shirley was called to give her evidence, which she did in a clear voice. Thankfully, she was not asked to give any opinions, and as she stepped down, she caught Neil's eye, and tried to encourage him with a smile. But Neil only gave her a slight nod.

Some of the workers testified as to the safety precautions they took, and members of the committee seemed to be taking notes, no doubt to decide on whether or not they were adequate.

Walter Maguire had someone to speak for him, pleading that he was not yet well enough for the ordeal. The poor condition of the site at that point was heavily underlined, but it was agreed that this was not unusual. Old buildings due to be demolished were often in a dangerous state.

It was also brought out that Neil had continued to pay Maguire's wages to his family, and Shirley thought this would be a point in his favour, then saw that it might be construed as an admission of responsibility.

Every question seemed to have two sides, she thought, despondently.

★   ★   ★

Finally, the committee retired to consider their verdict, and Shirley had a ridiculous desire to run up to Neil and insist on taking him home. He'd had enough, she thought worriedly.

Shouldn't someone have spoken up for the fine thing he was doing in Inverdorran? Couldn't they see that his courage and resourcefulness was going to mean jobs and money for other people? He was trying to do it so carefully, too, without spoiling any site of natural beauty.

No-one seems to appreciate Neil properly, Shirley thought, her heart full of compassion for him. Did no-one but herself realise what an ordeal it was, waiting for the committee to return with their findings?

Then, suddenly, they had all returned, and the chairman announced that they would like to consider it all further and would postpone their verdict. This would be communicated to them later.

Oh no! Shirley thought. Oh, poor Neil! How can he keep going without a decision being made?

Coming out of the building, she could see several people ahead of her, all wanting to talk to Neil. Geoffrey

Lewis was waiting to waylay her, and Shirley would like to have avoided him, and gone on to talk to Neil, but Geoffrey was looking quiet and subdued. He had intended to go as a witness for Maguire, but had obviously changed his mind.

She could see Catriona running up to take Neil's arm, and with a sigh of resignation, she slowed her step and turned to Geoffrey.

'Well? How did it go from your point of view?' she asked.

'None of us know yet, do we? But I just want you to know that I'm changing my mind about Fraser. I was wrong. I've learned a lot by talking to people about this, and trying to get them to see my point of view.

'Instead I've seen theirs, and I realise that Fraser is doing a fine thing for Inverdorran. That's an eyesore he's clearing away, and he's called in a good architect to landscape the complex. You can't just live on beauty and scenery — I realise that now. There's got to be work, too, and he's providing that. I can only hope it goes well for him.'

'I hope you'll tell him that,' Shirley said crisply. 'If you ask me, he needs all the encouragement he can get.'

She could see Catriona arguing furiously with Neil, then the girl turned away, her cheeks scarlet.

Neil stood for a moment looking round, then strode towards the waste ground where their cars had all been parked.

Shirley followed. Her own car was parked nearby, but she wanted a word with Neil before they drove home. Perhaps she could persuade him to take her for a cup of tea, though he was the one who needed it.

She was too late, however. As she neared the car park, she saw Neil's car begin to move slowly. She waved, but he did not appear to see her, and swung the car round to drive towards the street.

Suddenly, her heart seemed to freeze with terror as she saw Neil, his face ashen, slump forward on to the wheel of the car, which plunged forward out of control.

With a stifled scream, Shirley watched it career towards a wooden fence. Horrified, she listened to the splintering of wood, then the car plunged towards a grassy slope beyond.

'How Dare You Say That!'

Shirley was hardly aware that she was running towards Neil's car until she felt Geoffrey Lewis pulling her arm. All around her, people seemed to be running from all directions, but she and Geoffrey reached the car first.

'There's a fire risk, Shirley,' he told her, 'and besides — you'd better not look. Leave this to me.'

'I'm a doctor, remember?' she said brusquely, though there was a dull, sick feeling inside which had nothing to do with her medical training.

Geoffrey wrenched open the door, then ran round to the front of the car.

'Not much damage done,' he said. 'He's been lucky. That grassy slope would break his speed. It could have been that wall further down.'

Shirley hardly heard him. Neil had been thrown forward, but his seat-belt had saved him. She was pretty sure he had fainted before the car hit the grassy bank, and must have been completely relaxed.

Anxiously she examined him, being careful to disturb as little as possible, though she was relieved to hear the sirens of the police car, and later, the ambulance.

For once, Shirley was glad to have Geoffrey by her side, as she waited beside the car while the police took notes. From somewhere, he produced a flask of hot coffee, and she drank it gratefully. She had given Neil emergency treatment, and saw that he was wrapped carefully in a blanket.

'You go on home,' she told Geoffrey, 'while I go to the hospital with Neil, and if you'll explain things to Grandfather, I'll be most grateful. Don't alarm him, though.'

'I've got a better idea than that. I'll ring your home and say you've been delayed, and drive your car to the hospital. After that, I think I ought to drive you home. Maybe you're hardened to driving away from an accident, but I think in this case, you'd better not risk it. It's already been a gruelling day at that tribunal. Please take my advice.'

'Perhaps you're right, Geoffrey,' she agreed. 'I can tell Grandfather myself, when I get back.' She managed a smile. 'You seem to make a habit of driving my cars!'

'Don't I just! Never mind, I'll be taking you out in a large limousine of my own one of these days. Don't worry — I'm only teasing,' he added, seeing the wary look in her eyes.

Geoffrey admired Shirley Baxter more than any girl he had ever met, but he knew she was not for him.

How history seemed to repeat itself, Shirley thought, as she once again accompanied an accident patient to hospital. Last time it was Walter Maguire, but this time it was Neil, and she tried to pretend to herself that it was all routine. But although Neil had not been so badly injured, physically, as

Walter, Shirley could not still the niggle of worry which was eating into her. He was ill, even before the accident, she reminded herself. Neil had fainted, she believed, *before* the car crashed.

It seemed a long wait at the hospital before she eventually saw him safely tucked up in bed. The screens had been placed round, and he was already drowsy with drugs. Shirley had discussed his condition with the Casualty Officer, but now she was visiting Neil as a friend, not as a doctor.

'What happened, Shirley?' he was asking.

'A slight accident. Nothing to worry about, Neil,' she said reassuringly. 'You went the wrong way in your car.'

'But I — I can't stay here,' he protested weakly. 'The complex — I must see to things . . . '

'I'll go and see David, if you like,' Shirley told him. 'You won't be in here very long . . . just a few days. I'm sure David will be seeing to things for you.'

'Would you?' He managed a weak

smile and she could see him relaxing a little. 'Shirley, you're . . . '

She could not catch the last few muttered words as he dropped off to sleep. For a long moment she looked down at him, thinking he looked years younger with the grim, tense look removed from his face. Perhaps this enforced rest would go a long way to making Neil slow down and take things easier. Quietly she left the ward and went to find Geoffrey.

Shirley was surprised to find it was still fairly early. It seemed hours since they left the tribunal because so much had happened.

'I'll drop you off at the Sinclairs',' she said to Geoffrey, 'then go on to see David Fraser. I think I ought to tell them about Neil, and reassure them a little.'

'Well, if you're sure,' Geoffrey said, 'though I'd be happy to drive you there and walk back.'

'No need for that,' Shirley insisted, 'though I'm grateful to have you with me at the moment. We've all had a good shaking up, but I feel better now that Neil's in good hands.'

'He was lucky to have you near, Shirley, and to get expert medical attention straightaway. I often think those who choose to do medicine are of greatest benefit to society. I used to think that most important of all was to guide and train young minds.'

'We all have our part to play,' Shirley said, 'even Neil, whose project will mean work for a great many and healthy pursuits for a great many more.'

Geoffrey was silent for a moment. 'More power to his elbow,' he said at length.

★   ★   ★

Mrs Fraser was delighted to see Shirley, though her face sobered when she learned the reason for the visit.

'We've been expecting Neil any time, Dr Baxter,' she said. 'David is in here watching television. We've been anxious about the results of the tribunal, and hoping Neil would ring.'

As she conducted Shirley into the lounge, the two Fraser children, Jamie and Fiona, rushed towards her. She had been a favourite with them since she bandaged Jamie's knee. However, their mother sternly ordered them up to bed. David switched off the television.

'What happened?' he asked simply.

As briefly as she could, Shirley explained the circumstances, watching the concern expressed on David's face.

'Is he badly hurt?' he asked. 'I'd better get up there straightaway.'

'No need. You can telephone if you like. But he was lucky, David, and there are no bones broken. He'll be black and blue on his arms and chest for a while, and there is a small cut above his right eye, but we dealt with that very quickly. No, his greatest anxiety is for you to get on with the work at the complex.'

'Then you think the tribunal won't be too hard on us?'

Shirley bit her lip. 'I can't possibly

guess, David, but Neil won't go down without a fight, and he seems determined to keep going.'

'I know. It's like a fever with him. It's as though he sees a vision, and nothing will distract him from it. Sometimes I think he loves Inverdorran better than any of us. It was becoming a dying community and whereas there were those among us who lamented, Neil went one better and did something about it.'

'Will you be able to keep things going, David?' Shirley asked. 'If you can, Neil will be so relieved, I'm sure of that.'

'Of course I can,' said David. 'I'll soon nip up to the hospital to see him when I've got everything rolling.'

'I expect they'll send him home soon,' Shirley murmured. 'They're desperate for beds these days.'

She turned to Mrs Fraser.

'Will you be able to look after him here, Mrs Fraser?'

'Certainly I will, even if I have to get

help. This is Neil's home, you know, being the older brother, though he was wise enough to see that David can run the farm better than he, and to let him get on with it. I'll prepare his bedroom for him, though I hope you'll be calling to attend to him. We never seem to see the district nurse these days.'

'She has a wide area to cover,' Shirley said quietly, 'but you needn't worry. Neil doesn't have wounds which require attention. Rest is what he needs now.'

She drove the short distance home, feeling that she wanted to forgo supper and crawl quietly into bed. It had been the longest day of her life, except for that other day when she travelled up from London to Inverdorran all those weeks ago. London seemed so distant now. She really was very much at home here in Inverdorran, she thought, looking about her as she parked the car.

★ ★ ★

Shirley was about to go upstairs when Mrs Ross came hurrying out of the sitting-room.

'Oh, I'm so glad you're home, Miss Shirley,' she said. 'Miss Maxwell — Catriona — is here to see you. She's been waiting a wee while, and she says she's not going home till you come.'

'Oh.' Shirley's heart sank. She didn't feel like seeing Catriona at the moment, she was tired — all she wanted to do was sleep.

'Where's Grandfather?' she asked.

'Och, he went upstairs for a wee rest an hour or so ago. He said he'd see you when you got home.'

'I suppose I'd better see Catriona first.'

'I've kept your supper warm for you, Miss Shirley.'

'Oh, I shan't want much,' the girl said wearily. 'A snack will do.'

Catriona did not look like her usual carefully-groomed self. Her hair was wild, and there was no carefully-applied make-up on her face. In a way, she looked much more appealing to Shirley, until Catriona began to bombard her with questions.

'I saw there had been an accident, but I had no idea it was Neil,' she explained. 'I've just seen Geoffrey Lewis and he put me right. What happened, and where is he? I was so shaken up I forgot to ask Geoffrey, and he has gone out, so I came on here to you. You'll be able to tell me more, anyway.'

'I can't tell you much, Catriona,' Shirley said wearily. 'What a day it's been! Neil's car ran into a grassy slope.'

'Was he avoiding something — a child? A dog?'

'No. I suspect he fainted at the wheel.'

'Fainted?' Catriona leapt to her feet, white faced.

'He has been under a strain for a while,' Shirley pointed out, annoyed with herself for saying so much to Catriona. If she had not been so tired, she might have satisfied the other girl with a simpler explanation.

'I knew it,' Catriona said, almost triumphantly. 'Even if that tribunal doesn't ruin him, he'll *have* to give up now — on medical grounds! He isn't fit to keep that place going, is he?

'You can use your influence on him, can't you, Shirley? Professionally, I mean — to get him to give it up and go to Edinburgh. It's ridiculous for him to be hanging around in this — this backwater, when he could have a wonderful life — a wonderful future . . .'

'Stop, Catriona!' Shirley cried, amazed at the girl. She seemed to see nothing beyond her own interests and her own schemes. She was willing to turn anything to her own advantage, even Neil's accident!

'I have no intention of influencing Neil in this way,' she said, trying to control the anger in her voice. 'Neil must live his life as *he* wants, and I certainly won't be advising him to give up on medical grounds. I can only advise him in general terms, and let him decide how to act on that advice.'

'You're too mealy-mouthed,' Catriona cried, and the hot colour flooded Shirley's cheeks.

'How dare you say that!' she demanded. 'I'm trying to be patient with you, Catriona, but it's very hard. I saw you and Neil arguing just before he got into his car to drive away, and I saw how upset he was. I saw him slump forward in a faint, and I saw his car hit that grassy bank.

'It's more than likely that you contributed towards that accident by your own selfish attitude . . . ' She broke off as she saw the colour drain from the other girl's face, and as she realised what she was saying.

'I — I'm sorry, Catriona,' she said huskily. 'That was unforgivable of me.'

'I should think it was,' retorted Catriona in a high, brittle voice. 'How unfair can you get, accusing me of — of causing Neil's accident! Why, he might have been killed! But I know what it is . . . '

Her voice seemed to rise in pitch so that it screamed into Shirley's head.

'You want Neil for yourself. That's what it is! You want him to stay here — with you! You don't want him to go to Edinburgh. You'd rather see him slaving away here, all his life, in Inverdorran, with you creeping around him, all sweetness and light. *You* want him!'

Catriona threw the last words over her shoulder as she rushed to the door, banging it behind her.

Shirley's knees were trembling as she stood, feeling even more shocked than she had been at any time during that long day.

She wanted to run after Catriona and deny all the charges, yet she couldn't. Something was finding an echo in her heart. Again she felt the horror of seeing the car plunge forward, with Neil at the wheel, and again she remembered standing beside the hospital bed, looking down at his dark face smoothed out in sleep.

Something had stirred in her then, and was finding an echo now. She *did* care for Neil. He was beginning to mean more to her than any man she had ever known. The knowledge left her sick and shaken, so that her face was ashen when her grandfather walked slowly into the room.

'What was all that about?' he asked.

'It — it was Catriona Maxwell. We've had a row,' she said simply.

Old Dr Baxter looked at his granddaughter, seeing that tears were not far away. Shirley probably hated rows as much as he did himself, and found them upsetting.

It was a pity, too, that it was Maxwell's daughter. He felt he owed the Brigadier a big favour for being so good with his roses, and recently he had been coming round to give him a good game of chess. In fact, he was enjoying Maxwell's company again, and his daughter seemed to be a nice enough girl, if a bit brittle.

Some young women were inclined to

put on that kind of shell when they were growing up, but usually the real person broke through once they'd made a happy marriage.

Shirley should be more perceptive . . .

'Wouldn't you like to tell me about it, Shirley?' he asked, sitting down. He wanted to get to the bottom of this, and watched while Shirley wiped her nose and mouth, with a handkerchief. The girl looked very tired.

'We quarrelled about Neil Fraser,' she said, after a while, and began to tell the old doctor all about it, though she kept the final part of the quarrel to herself, merely saying that Catriona thought she had her own reasons for not supporting her.

Luckily old Dr Baxter was more concerned with the medical aspect of it all, than the personal one.

'Neil's been under strain for a while then, Shirley?' he asked, frowning. 'I was wondering why he hadn't even come round to see me recently.'

'I think he's been keyed up about this accident to Walter Maguire,' she said. 'From what David said, they're very finely balanced between the budget and the schedule. They can't afford anything which would rock the boat too much. So the tribunal is of prime importance. I think the fact that there was no decision after he'd been all keyed up waiting for it, was the last straw, added to which he . . .'

She decided not to say that he'd had words with Catriona, and saw that her grandfather was now concentrating on all she had told him, plus details of the accident.

Mrs Ross had brought her a nourishing snack on a tray, and Shirley was now eating it. Her grandfather watched her in silence, thinking it was one night when Shirley could use a good night's sleep.

With regard to Neil Fraser, he found himself toying with the problem, pretty much as he had done before his illness, and calling on his long years of experience as well as his training. He had always kept abreast of new methods, and weighed them up together with his own findings. When Neil Fraser came home, he himself was going to take on the case, Dr Baxter decided. It might stop Catriona and Shirley rowing over him anyway!

*   *   *

Dr Brian Wills drove up to Beech House a few days later in a brand-new sports car, and Shirley rushed out to meet him. From the window, her grandfather watched the young man leaping out of the car and swinging Shirley off her feet, then he placed his arm companionably round her shoulders as they walked indoors together.

'You must be doing well,' Shirley teased him. 'That's some car.'

'Not mine,' he said regretfully. 'I'm still overworked and underpaid, but my brother has gone to Canada on a business trip and has lent me his car.

He manufactures paper clips,' he added ruefully.

'Never mind, you'll be a consultant one day,' said Shirley, and introduced him to her grandfather.

The old man liked the look of Shirley's young friend, seeing his pleasant open face and warm smile.

'You're very welcome, Dr Wills,' he said courteously.

'I'm happy to be here, sir. Inverdorran is a lovely quiet place after London. I'll be able to catch up on some of my thinking.'

'Some of your walking, too, I hope,' Shirley said, 'and some of your eating. Mrs Ross has made us an enormous tea.'

'Now you're talking!' Brian enthused. 'Do you remember some of the snatched meals we had in London, Shirley? Beans on toast used to taste delicious.'

'Bread and jam tasted wonderful too.' Shirley laughed. 'Tell me how everybody is.'

As they sat down to Mrs Ross's generous tea, she and Brian tried to remember to bring her grandfather into the conversation, but sooner or later Shirley would ask about yet another old friend.

'What about Molly Porter?'

'She went to Guy's.'

'And Mr Fenton?'

'Still performing miracles in brain surgery. He's so diffident, but once he gets to the operating table . . . '

Dr Baxter watched the two young people talking with animation, and there was a strange feeling of loneliness in his heart. This was part of Shirley's life which he could not share. Some day she might even want to go back.

Dr Baxter looked at his empty plate, and pushed it away. He was beginning to depend very much on his young granddaughter, and it was a mistake. He ought to be encouraging her to lead her own life.

Perhaps he ought to encourage her to go back to London, or even to her own people — Colin, his son, and Kate, the daughter-in-law he had never even seen . . . if she had no plans for settling down here. They must miss her a great deal. It was very hard not to want to hang on to her, he thought with a sigh.

'How's Leila?' Shirley was asking, and this time Brian seemed to take longer to reply.

'Very well,' he said at length. 'She — she sends her love.'

'I've a lot to thank her for,' Shirley said, then coloured as she saw her grandfather's eyes on her. Sometime she would tell him all about her lapse, when she was ready to give up medicine, but not just yet. He was now going out more on his own, but not back to normal just yet.

★ ★ ★

It was fun to take Brian walking round Inverdorran and she was surprised by the number of people she was able to introduce to him. She saw him looking at her with speculation, and the glint of humour was in her eyes when old Mr Elliot wrung him warmly by the hand.

'So this is your young man from London, Dr Shirley,' he said. 'You're very welcome, young man.'

'Dr Wills,' Shirley said quickly.

'Another doctor,' Mr Elliot said with pleasure. He was in praise of doctors at present, still heartily satisfied with the way they had put him on to his feet again, after months of keeping his pain and sickness to himself.

'Oh dear, it'll be all over Inverdorran that you're my young man from London,' Shirley said, her eyes glinting with fun.

Brian's eyes were thoughtful, however.

'You seem to know everybody,' he said. 'Do you feel you've carved yourself a niche? Will you be taking over from your grandfather — when he retires, I mean?'

'I don't know,' Shirley said, and could not stop her thoughts going to

Neil. Perhaps Neil didn't care about her, but already she was beginning to realise she only really cared about one man, and if he did not see things that way, then there was only her career left.

She could see now that her feelings for Ian Andrews had stemmed from her gratitude for the reassurance and help he gave her during that particularly difficult time in her career. She had grasped at Ian as a child might grasp at a parent or guardian, but it had not been real love.

'I've been putting off making plans till Grandfather was better,' she said.

'He seems fine now.'

'Oh, he is. Another week or two and he'll be completely recovered. He's a strong man for his age.'

Two days later, Mrs Fraser rang up to say that David had gone to collect Neil from hospital and they were now home. Neil had brought a letter for his GP but he was still confined to bed.

'I should think he is,' said Shirley. 'I'll come round this . . . ' she hesitated, remembering plans she and Brian had made for that evening ' . . . in the morning to see him, and I'll collect the letter then.'

She put down the telephone, resisting the impulse to rush off to the Frasers right there and then. Shirley walked away slowly. She had made rather a fool of herself over Ian Andrews, and that was a lesson to her. She mustn't make the same mistake with Neil.

★　★　★

Nevertheless, her heart beat more rapidly as she drove towards the Frasers' farm the following day, and got out of the car to ring the bell. Everything was quiet, and she knew the children would be at school, though Mrs Fraser was bound to be at home, to look after Neil.

But when the door opened, Shirley found herself staring at a very pretty girl with soft, curling brown hair and pansy-brown eyes.

'Yes?' she asked.

'I'm Dr Baxter,' said Shirley. 'I've called to see Mr Fraser.'

'Oh, do come in,' the girl said. 'We've been expecting you, Dr Baxter — though I hadn't quite expected . . .' She looked confused. 'I'm Joan Gibson, Ellen's sister.'

'Ellen?'

'Yes. My sister is married to David Fraser.'

'But of course,' said Shirley. 'Stupid of me.'

There had been a faint resemblance to someone, and she could see now that it was Mrs Fraser.

'I haven't been here very long,' Joan Gibson was saying, 'but I'll soon get things sorted out and get into uniform. I'm a nurse. I trained at the Western in Edinburgh.' She grinned impishly. 'Neil tends to forget I'm a nurse unless I wear it. I can make him behave if I look a bit more official.'

Shirley tried to laugh with her, but

there was a stiffness in her. There had been a wealth of tenderness in Joan Gibson's voice when she spoke of Neil. They must have known one another for years, thought Shirley, and she had rarely seen a lovelier girl.

She was ashamed of the deep well of jealousy inside her, so that her professional manner was even more brisk than usual when she walked into Neil's bedroom.

He was looking a great deal brighter than the last time she had seen him, but he still seemed pale and rather haggard.

'I hope I don't have to stay here very long, Shirley,' Neil said, with a smile which faded a little as she found it hard to respond.

'Give me that letter, and we shall see,' she said crisply, and had some difficulty in concentrating on the official report. She was so used to seeing him striding about looking purposeful and even forbidding. But now his very helplessness made her heart jerk, and she longed to smooth back the dark hair from his forehead.

'I'm afraid you're in there for a few more days yet, Neil,' she said, as she made a routine examination, then glanced at her watch.

'Do you have to go rushing off?' he asked. 'Can't you stay and talk to me, just for a moment?'

She shook her head, avoiding his eyes, then changed her mind.

'What is it? Are you worried about anything?'

She saw the hooded look in his eyes again. Shirley only seemed able to talk about medical matters. Girls seemed to grow an extra shell when they became doctors.

'Thank you for what you did for me,' he said politely. 'I'm still waiting to hear from the tribunal, but otherwise everything's being cared for. David and my foreman are seeing to that.'

'That's fine,' she said awkwardly, very much aware of Joan Gibson in the background. She rose to her feet again.

'If you feel any pain at all, or

sickness, I'll come at once, but I think you'll be on your feet in a few more days. You must try not to worry, that's all.'

He stared at her broodingly, then nodded.

'I'll be OK. You'd better go heal the sick. I believe you have a friend up from London?'

She nodded. 'We were colleagues. I'll see you again, Neil — perhaps tomorrow.'

Joan hurried downstairs to show her out, and to assure Shirley that she'd see Neil took his tablets.

'It's so nice to have met you,' she said shyly. 'The family have talked of you such a lot.'

Shirley smiled and nodded, thinking that Joan was an entirely different sort of girl from Catriona. Catriona did not deserve Neil, but Joan was clever and competent, as well as pretty, and she suspected that the young girl thought very highly of him.

She was still deep in thought when

she arrived home, to find Brian and her grandfather removing their coats.

'We've been for a splendid walk,' Brian said, his face glowing with fresh air.

'Yes, we're both famished.' Dr Baxter grinned, and went off towards the kitchen to find Mrs Ross.

Brian turned to Shirley.

'You look tired,' he said. 'Been finding things a bit much?'

She shrugged. 'Perhaps, a little.'

'Then why not come for a walk with me after tea?' he urged. 'There's something I want to discuss with you.'

A Cry For Help

Shirley sat opposite her grandfather and Brian at the small tea table which Mrs Ross had set in front of the fire in the lounge. She was uneasily aware that Brian might have read more into their friendship than she had intended. He had always been warmly sympathetic towards her, but she had considered him to be one friend she could rely on without any complications.

Now she feared that she might have been wrong over this, just when she could do without more trouble than she had already.

'You're very quiet, Shirley,' Dr Baxter said, breaking into her thoughts. 'Not worried about anything, are you?'

She shot a quick glance at Brian, who turned to smile at her warmly.

'It's Neil Fraser,' she said at length. 'I'm not happy about him at all,

225

Grandfather. He was run-down before the accident, and his blood count is low. But it isn't only that. He — he was under such a strain, and it doesn't seem to be easing. I wish he'd get some good news from that tribunal. I'm sure that would help.'

'Hmm.' Dr Baxter pressed his finger-tips together, thoughtfully, his eyes on Shirley's worried face. 'I think this is one case I'd better deal with myself, Shirley,' he said. 'I've known the Frasers since they were boys, and I want to go into all this with Neil myself.'

When her grandfather used that tone of voice, Shirley knew it was wise not to argue. Yet she'd had an aching sense of loss when he said he would look after Neil. In one way it would be a relief not to have to see him, but in another she was going to miss popping in to check up on his health.

Then there was Joan Gibson. Thinking about the pretty, cheerful young nurse, Shirley had to admit it was her own jealousy which had led her to suppose there was anything special about her friendship with Neil. Yet how did Neil feel about her? He had never given any hint that she meant more to him than a casual friend.

She picked at her food, crumbling a scone on her plate, until Mrs Ross arrived to clear it up. She was about to chide Shirley on wasting good food, but a look at the girl's face stilled her tongue.

Miss Shirley had something on her mind, Mrs Ross decided.

'Would you like me to make you some more hot tea?' she asked.

'No, thank you, Mrs Ross. That was lovely.'

'And besides, she's going for a walk with me,' Brian said firmly, getting to his feet.

With a sigh, Shirley also rose from the table. There was no use evading the issue.

'Let's go down the side of this field to the river bank,' Brian suggested, 'and we can sit beside that fisherman's hut.

It's nice and secluded at this time of year.'

'All right,' Shirley agreed, and strode along beside him, leaping over a stile at the bottom of the field.

'It's lovely in here,' Brian said when they had reached the old wooden hut, 'with only the murmur of the river to disturb the peace, and the birds singing their hearts out. Your grandfather and I watched a kingfisher fishing away from that branch yesterday.

'It is one precious memory I'm going to take back to London with me. If I haven't thanked you before for this wonderful break, then I'm thanking you now, Shirley. I really do feel energetic enough to start again.'

'I'm glad of that.' She smiled. 'I know what a strain hospital life can be after a while.'

Brian nodded. 'Yes, I — I was rather hoping to talk to you about that. Are you really settled in Inverdorran, Shirley? Don't you ever miss the old life?'

She looked at him warily. 'In what way, Brian?'

'Oh, the general bustle of a big hospital, and all the fine work you used to do. And it was fine work, until you overdid it. I suppose you realise that now, looking back?'

Shirley nodded.

'Well, you seem to have put it all behind you now,' Brian went on. 'So when I heard Tom Fletcher was going to a consultant's position in Birmingham, I thought of you. You could do Tom's job, Shirley, and you'd be part of the hospital team again.'

Shirley's cheeks were flushing. Tom Fletcher held down a very good position and was much respected.

'When is he going?' she asked.

'You'd have until the end of the month to apply. I think you should,' said Brian eagerly.

'Three more weeks,' Shirley mused.

'Do think about it, Shirley. We'd all like to see you back, especially Leila . . . You remember Leila, don't you?'

Shirley shot a keen glance at Brian, then she relaxed, smiling.

'You're in love with Leila?' she asked.

Brian coloured rosily. 'Well — yes I am, but I — I'm not sure about Leila. She's very attractive, isn't she? And she's got such a lot of friends.'

'Faint heart never won fair lady! I think you ought to take a chance on it, Brian.'

'Will you also take a chance on the job?' he asked.

Shirley grew pensive. 'I'll have to consider it carefully,' she said. 'There's Grandfather, for a start.'

'He's as strong as I am. You should have seen him galloping over the fields today!'

'Yes, but there's the practice, and one thing and another,' she ended lamely. She could hardly tell Brian all about Neil Fraser!

'Come on, let's go home,' Brian said, tucking her hand into his arm. 'You're tired now.'

⋆ ⋆ ⋆

The following morning, Shirley saw Brian away in his car, after breakfast.

'You know, I've probably enjoyed your holiday as much as you have,' she said.

'I can't believe it's over.' Brian sighed. 'Though it will be nice to see . . . Well — to see Leila again.'

'Give her my love.'

'I will. Don't forget what I told you, though it's a good idea to consider it carefully. That way you're more sure of leaping in the right direction. Let me know, won't you, whatever you decide to do, after you've thought it over?'

Shirley nodded. 'Don't worry. I'll let you have my decision as soon as possible.'

She stood back as her grandfather appeared to wave Brian away. He was all set to go to work, and paused on the step as Brian bumped his way out of the gate, before going to get his own car out of the garage. Shirley had disappeared indoors, but her final conversation with Brian Wills was still in the old man's mind.

What decision, he wondered. Surely it could be nothing but whether or not to accept a proposal of marriage! Dr Baxter's brows wrinkled thoughtfully. Brian Wills was a fine young man, but did he really want him to take Shirley away back to London?

★ ★ ★

Dr Baxter's mind was still on this when he got out of the car at the Frasers', and briskly climbed up the steps to the front door. He had been told about the young nurse who had come to look after Neil, and was pleased with her neat, competent appearance, as Joan Gibson answered the door.

'Dr Baxter, Senior,' he announced himself.

'Come in, Doctor,' Joan said, and quietly led the way up to Neil's bedroom.

As soon as he set eyes on the young man, Dr Baxter could understand Shirley's misgivings. His face was pale and drawn, the eyes luminous.

'Where's Shirley?' Neil asked, as the older man proceeded to examine him thoroughly, finding little wrong with his patient physically that a rest and good tonic could not cure — or so he hoped.

'Seeing off young Dr Wills. His holiday is finished, and he's away back to London.'

'Oh,' Neil said, leaning back on his pillows as though with relief.

'You're going to need to relax a bit more,' the old doctor said. 'You're as tight as a drum. Has your head been bothering you?'

'Just a bit,' Neil admitted. 'Is he a special friend of Shirley's . . . Dr Wills, I mean?'

'Put your hand out and spread out your fingers, like so.'

Neil did so, his fingers trembling a little.

'Uh-huh . . . What was that? Oh, young Dr Wills . . . Yes, well . . . '
Dr Baxter's fears came rushing back, and it was easy to see by his face that he was concerned.

Neil felt as though a great weight was pressing down on him as he lay back wearily on to his pillow, his eyes dulled again.

'I'll give him something extra, Nurse Gibson,' the doctor said, taking out his prescription booklet. 'See if this picks him up a bit. You seem to be coping, however.'

'He's not the easiest of patients,' said Joan, her eyes laughing, but Neil did not respond.

'You should come and join the district nurses,' Dr Baxter told her. 'We're short of nurses at the moment. Sometimes Shirley has to do jobs that a good district nurse could manage easily.'

'I just might take you up on that, Doctor.'

Shirley was out when Dr Baxter got home after a number of morning calls. He felt tired, but happy, thankful to be back in the saddle again. He was also pleased and proud to know that Shirley had won her own special place in the hearts of the local people.

It was now nearing the date for Ian Andrews' wedding in Edinburgh, and Shirley was repaying the favour Ian had done for them when her grandfather was so ill, by seeing to a number of Ian's patients while he attended to a great many personal matters.

Alterations were being made to the house, and one or two rooms were being redecorated. Ian wanted to be on hand to supervise this and Shirley had offered to take on some of his work.

'I can manage it,' she said cheerfully, 'Grandfather has practically sacked me as it is.'

'Nonsense. If I didn't have you, I'd have to get someone else,' Dr Baxter told her. Shirley's eyes grew thoughtful, even as she smiled. Would her grandfather really miss her if she went to London? Was she really still needed here in Inverdorran?

'Though, of course, you mustn't let me stand in your way, if you — well — want to do anything special,' the old man added hastily. That was how he had lost Colin, by trying to hang on to him! He must not make the same mistake with Shirley.

But Shirley felt unreasonably hurt, deep inside. What did her grandfather *really* want? Was he telling her she was free to go, now he was better? The thought made her feel saddened, and somehow insecure.

Yet she knew Ian needed her help at the moment, and she was kept very busy with patients living in outlying districts.

Hannah McEwan at the General Store had bad varicose veins, and Shirley made a note to see if something could be done for her in hospital.

Nor did she like the look of Andrew Graham who worked on a farm farther up the valley. The herd of cattle were accredited, and none of the other farm hands had shown any sign of illness and yet Shirley had not yet ruled out brucellosis.

'He gets very depressed at times, and

he seems to get a bit feverish, Doctor,' Mrs Graham said to Shirley.

'Yes, well . . . I'll have a word with Dr Andrews, but I'm sure something can be done to make you feel better soon, Mr Graham.'

She was getting more used to a country practice, and took all the travelling in her stride.

When she reached Beech House, she found her grandfather sitting reading the daily paper. He looked very fit and well, his eyes keen and shrewd as he lowered his paper to look at her.

'Mind if you go up the valley, Shirley. There's to be heavy rain and the river can rise quickly. The Dorran Bridge isn't too stable. It's due to be rebuilt, but the last floods gave it a crack or two. I've been up in arms about it before now.'

'I've just come from there, Grandfather,' said Shirley. 'I'll have a word with Ian, but I think Andrew Graham has brucellosis. He might have had it for a while.'

'There's been a few cases,' her grandfather admitted. 'By the way, have you seen young Catriona recently?'

'No,' she said. 'Not recently.'

'Her father is coming round to play chess with me this evening.'

'Excellent,' said Shirley, then decided to take the bull by the horns. 'How's Neil?'

Dr Baxter drew a deep breath, then sighed. 'I could see what was worrying you about him, Shirley. His nerves are finely stretched. He's got himself into a fine state trying to put this place on its feet. I'm trying something new,' he added, going into technical details. 'That should slow him down, and give him time to think, then we can maybe do something with him.'

'Yes . . . could do,' Shirley said, nodding.

'He's got a good nurse anyway,' her grandfather went on. 'Mrs Fraser's young sister, Joan Gibson. She's a good, competent young woman. I was telling her we could do with her joining the ranks of the district nurses.'

'What did she say to that?' Shirley asked.

'Oh, she was interested, very interested. She's just the kind of young woman you want.'

'Yes, she is,' Shirley agreed.

So Joan was interested in working locally! Again she thought of the girl's affectionate smile when she talked about Neil. She could hardly help falling in love with him, thought Shirley. In his weakened state, he would be even more endearing to her, and she must surely admire all the work he was trying to do.

Shirley fought against a wave of jealousy, deliberately turning her mind to other things.

'Ian has a locum coming for the two weeks he'll be away on his honeymoon,' she said, 'but I think he's hoping I'll be able to help out as well with taking surgery, and visiting some of the outlying farms.'

Dr Baxter nodded, though it was Shirley he was thinking about, not Ian

Andrews. At least she had got over her infatuation for him, because surely that was what it had been!

Now, whether she realised it or not, she was talking about Ian quite naturally without the strained note in her voice. Perhaps young Dr Wills was responsible for that!

★　★　★

The following Saturday, Shirley set out early for the drive to Edinburgh to attend Ian and Alison's wedding.

Shirley had been glad of a boost to her morale from Mrs Ross, then her grandfather, when she appeared round the kitchen door wearing the lovely misty-blue suit.

'Oh, Miss Shirley, but you do look lovely,' said Mrs Ross. 'It seems to bring out such a nice colour in your cheeks.'

'Thank you, Mrs Ross.' Shirley laughed. 'But I think I got that from tramping round the farms, or walking up to the General Store. I didn't have this colour in London.'

'Och, you're far better back home here in Inverdorran,' Mrs Ross said, and Shirley was reminded once again that this was a decision she would soon have to make.

Old Dr Baxter padded in from his garden. They were only taking emergency calls that day, and he was taking time off to keep an eye on his roses. He must not lose the good work Brigadier Maxwell had done.

He stopped short when he saw Shirley dressed up, then came forward slowly.

'You look beautiful, my dear. I just wish . . . '

'What?'

'That your father — your parents could see you now,' he said with a heart-felt sigh.

'Yes, it would be lovely to see Mum and Dad again.'

But there was no time for further discussion as Shirley glanced at the hall clock as she walked towards the front door, picking up her new handbag which exactly matched her blue shoes.

'I'll see you tonight then, Grandfather. Don't forget, if you need me you can ring the hotel where the reception is being held, but I don't think I'll be very late.'

'I'll be fine. Just have yourself a lovely day, and wish the young couple well for me.'

'You've already done that with the beautiful silver you bought them for a wedding gift,' said Shirley, and waved cheerfully as she climbed into the car.

★   ★   ★

The church was quiet and peaceful and rich with beautiful flowers. Shirley found herself relaxing and looking round at the many guests. She was sitting next to another GP, an old friend of Ian's, with his wife and two small children whose comments in a stage whisper made Shirley smile with amusement.

Then the organist began to play 'The Wedding March,' and Alison seemed to float down the aisle in a dress of flowing chiffon and lace, which suited her small dainty figure to perfection. She had chosen to be a traditional bride, and her young bridesmaid, a cousin, also looked beautiful in palest pink and lavender. Her solicitor father was tall with grey hair, and the lady in rose pink, sitting in the front pew, was no doubt his new wife.

Shirley felt her heart swelling with emotion as she looked at the young couple, so sure of their love, and of their future together. Yet her thoughts kept returning again and again to Neil, thinking of his strained appearance, and the fight he was having to put up in order to return to full health, as well as establishing the sports centre.

If only she had the right to fight by his side, Shirley thought longingly. Was it better for her to stay in Inverdorran, and hope she could help Neil, unobtrusively, in whatever way she could, or was it better to leave quietly, and return to London? The hospital job would appeal to her if she wanted to pursue her career, and if she tried hard enough, she knew she just might be accepted for the position.

And what about her grandfather? Shrewdly she suspected that he wanted her to be free to make her own mind up, but he would miss her if she went.

She rose as the bridal party walked up the aisle, Alison looking radiantly beautiful. Shirley had brought along a small camera, and took her own pictures to show her grandfather. She would send some home to her parents in New Zealand.

Later, at the reception, she was welcomed by the new Mrs Grant and her husband, and she thought that Alison's stepmother still looked like a bride herself. How marvellous to be so happy, Shirley thought rather wistfully, looking from Mrs Grant to the new Mrs Andrews.

The wedding breakfast was an elaborate affair with amusing speeches, then later Shirley had a chance to talk to Ian and Alison before she left for home.

'Aren't you going to stay for the dance?' Alison asked.

'No, I have a fairly long drive ahead of me,' Shirley said, 'so I'd better not leave it too late. I'll think about you, though, and you'll have to dance a waltz together for me.'

She kissed Alison and wished her happiness, then turned to Ian.

'It's been a lovely wedding. I know you'll both be very happy.'

He searched her face, seeing that she truly meant her good wishes. Yet there was a sad, lost look in her eyes, and fervently Ian Andrews wished that she, too, could find happiness.

'Thank you, my dear,' he said quietly. 'Give my regards to Dr Baxter. We'll be home soon.'

'Don't hurry — we're coping.'

Shirley grinned, and quietly left the hotel.

The drive home seemed much longer than the drive to Edinburgh, but at last she was passing Jock Sinclair's petrol station and garage, and she smiled, knowing she was almost home. How I love it, Shirley thought. If only I never have to leave it! She used to think that nowhere on earth could be more beautiful than her home in New Zealand, but it was Inverdorran which held her heart.

* * *

Shirley had the photographs she had taken of Ian's wedding developed as soon as possible, and collected them one afternoon after she had finished her calls.

Her grandfather and Mrs Ross were delighted to see them when she arrived home, and spread them out on the polished table in the lounge.

'She's such a dainty wee thing,' Mrs

Ross said admiringly, looking at the pretty bride, 'and that's a real picture-book dress. Oh, she's just like a princess.'

'She is indeed,' Shirley agreed. 'Look at this one of Ian, Grandfather. I caught him at an 'off' moment after the meal at the hotel!'

There were chuckles all round, then Mrs Ross pounced on one of Shirley, congratulating the bride and 'groom.

'Now, that's just lovely. I'm glad there's one of you, Miss Shirley.'

'One of the guests took it for me,' she smiled. 'I'll send them on to Mum and Dad . . . ' She paused, looking thoughtfully at her grandfather. 'It's odd, but we don't seem to have heard from them for a while.'

Then she could have bitten her tongue out when she saw the concern in his face.

'Ay, the same thought has been on my mind. You — you don't suppose Colin isn't too well again?'

She managed to laugh naturally. 'No,

I don't suppose it's that at all. I know my family, and a lazier lot with the pen, when they all become busy with other things, could not be found.

'Mother does try to keep writing, but I don't think she worries about me so much now that I'm here in Inverdorran with you. It was different in London.'

'No, I see what you mean,' Dr Baxter said, pleased.

Shirley turned away, though she had failed to convince herself with her own arguments. Her mother did not allow a long time to elapse without a message of some kind, even if she bullied Paul or Nancy into writing it. And it was a fairly quiet time at the moment, between lambing and shearing.

Uneasily Shirley felt that something was wrong, but she dared not let her grandfather see that she was worried, though her heart ached for news.

After tea, Dr Baxter put on his coat, coming in for a word with Shirley.

'I'm going round to the Maxwells' to

play chess,' he said. 'I won't be late, my dear. I know you won't allow me to stay up till all hours.'

'I'm only too happy to see you going out, Grandfather.' Shirley smiled.

She, herself, seemed to go out rarely for social occasions these days, she thought, with a sigh. Yet she had no heart in going out on her own.

It was an hour later when the telephone rang and she picked it up almost mechanically. It was Mrs Fraser.

'Hello. Is that Dr Baxter?'

'Speaking,' said Shirley.

'Oh, Doctor, I — I've been wondering what I ought to do. Joan has gone home for a couple of days, you see. Neil's been a lot better and was getting up to sit in a chair, in fact, but I've been worried about him this afternoon.'

'Oh?' Shirley's voice sounded hoarse.

'Yes, a letter came for him and I completely forgot to take it up to him until a short time ago. I think it was an official sort of letter, and when I went upstairs with his tea, Neil looked sort of funny. I didn't like the look of him, Dr Shirley. Do you think you could come right away?'

'I Lost My Nerve'

Shirley put down the telephone, her brows wrinkled anxiously. Mrs Fraser had sounded very worried about Neil and she, herself, did not like the sound of things.

Pausing only for a quick word with Mrs Ross, she hurried out to the car and drove the short distance to the Frasers' farm. On her way, she passed the building site of the sports centre and was surprised by the great strides which had been made. The place really looked like something now.

Mrs Fraser was already at the door, waiting for her, and Shirley lost no time in running up to the bedroom. Neil lay on the bed, his face pallid, the letter Mrs Fraser had mentioned crushed in his hand. So the news is bad, Shirley thought, with sinking heart.

Hurrying over to the bed, she took

his hand in hers.

'It isn't the end of the world, Neil. Even if Walter Maguire has won, and you're going to have a setback, things are so well forward now . . . '

He stared at her, dully. 'It's all right. The news is good — good news, Shirley. It's just that — it's taken so long . . . '

'Can I read it?' she asked, and saw that her hands were shaking as he handed her the letter. The tribunal had found that Walter Maguire had been largely responsible for his own accident, but went on to suggest very stringent measures so that the same thing could not happen again.

'But this is wonderful,' Shirley said.

She waited for a response from Neil, but there was none, and Shirley sat down on the bed.

'You'll have to pull yourself together, Neil, or if you can't, I'll have to arrange for you to see another — another kind of specialist.'

'A psychiatrist, you mean?' he asked.

'I don't think it need come to that. You've had a hard time, but it's over now, and you should see that sports complex! It looks terrific!'

'You've seen it?'

'Just now, on my way here. The men are all going flat out to get the place finished. David is no doubt doing his best, but he isn't you, Neil. It's you that so many people depend upon. Don't you remember how glorious it was going to be, giving work to so many people? Don't you remember all the marvellous plans you made, that day you showed me over the site and explained it all to me?'

He nodded. 'I remember.'

'Then can't you hold on to that? I know your mind must be tired, but try to think and plan, a little at a time. It will soon come. Just take one very small part of it, and build on that because that's how the sports complex got built in the first place.'

He was staring at her and she could see the dull look beginning to fade from his eyes, even as he began to move restlessly in bed. If only she could keep up his interest . . .

'It matters such a lot to a great many people.' She smiled eagerly. 'It even matters to me.'

'To you?' He was reaching out with his hand to take hold of hers, when there was a discreet knock on the door.

Shirley had been so concerned about instilling some life into Neil that she had been oblivious to all other noises. But now as Mrs Fraser opened the door, she saw that her grandfather was bringing up the rear.

Shirley got up awkwardly.

'Mrs Ross told me you were here,' he said.

'Yes, I . . . You were out when Mrs Fraser's call came, Grandfather,' she said, 'but I thought I'd better come myself. Neil has had news from the tribunal, but it's good news.'

'Good news, is it? Splendid! Then you've nothing to worry about, lad. Now, sit up in bed, and I'll give you a good going-over.'

He turned to Shirley. 'Yes, Mrs Ross said you'd taken the call when I got back from my chess game.'

Neil was looking from one to the other, a touch more colour in his face. Dr Baxter was listening to his chest and lungs, then his heart, and was peering into his eyes. He pulled his stethoscope from his ears.

'You'll live to be a hundred,' he said. 'All you need is a good wee holiday away from here. You're too much on top of your problems, but if you view them from a distance, then they'll fall into perspective. Where would you like to go?'

'Oh, I don't know.' Neil said wearily. 'Anywhere.'

'I don't think it's a good idea for him to go away to some holiday resort on his own,' Shirley said. He might just start brooding, she thought, and worrying. If only he could get the complex opened!

'What about Edinburgh?' Mrs Fraser

asked eagerly. 'There is plenty of room at my parents' home, and Joan would be there to look after him, and take him about. She would see to it that he didn't overdo things, but she wouldn't have him skulking at home either.'

'That's a splendid idea,' said Dr Baxter. 'The sooner the better.'

'Well, Joan is coming here tonight, and she could drive Neil to Edinburgh tomorrow. I could ring up my parents straightaway.'

'Couldn't be better. What do you think about that, Neil?'

Neil's eyes were on Shirley, then he looked away. 'If that's what you recommend, then I'll be happy to go.'

'Right. Come on then, Shirley,' said the old doctor. 'It's time we went home. Don't worry, my lad, you'll be fine.'

★ ★ ★

That night, Shirley could not sleep for thinking about Neil and she buried her flushed cheeks into the pillow. She could hear herself telling him how much it mattered to her, and wondered if she had again been guilty of wearing her heart on her sleeve.

When would she ever learn to have a bit of pride?

'You look as though a day in bed yourself wouldn't hurt you,' said her grandfather the following morning.

'Well, I can't spare the time,' she said. 'I'm going over to Ian's to have a word with his locum, Dr Ferguson. Ian introduced us at the wedding.'

'You'd better invite him to supper, then,' said Dr Baxter. 'We must show hospitality to a colleague.'

'Oh, all right, but I'd best have a word with Mrs Ross first of all.'

Dr Baxter shot her a glance. 'You're a bit miserable with yourself today. I hope you aren't sickening for a cold, or something.'

'I'm perfectly well.'

'Then there's something on your mind, my lass. Come on now, you might as well tell me about it.'

Shirley bit her lip. This time her feelings ran too deep and she felt she could not discuss Neil with her grandfather. She glanced at the mail, hoping for a letter from home. It seemed weeks since she had heard. 'Still no word from home,' she said thoughtfully.

So that was it! thought Dr Baxter. She was missing her own folks. He had never really encouraged her to talk much about her life in New Zealand. Somehow the less he knew of it, the better, since deep down he had always been hoping that Colin would come home again, one day.

'What's it like — in New Zealand, I mean?' he asked warily.

'You mean, what is the country like?'

'Yes. And the people, I suppose. What kind of life did you live? What's your home like?'

'Oh, wide and low-set . . . Plenty of rooms and lots and lots of flowers . . . '

'Such as?'

'Oh, cineraria, alyssum, ranunculas,

like here, and spring flowers like daffodils, primroses, and violets. Farther up from us is hilly country, with glorious waterfalls and bush country, with silver beeches and red beeches, and black pines, and red pines. I — I'm not good at descriptions. You'd have to go and see for yourself.'

'I'm not likely to be gallivanting all that way at my age,' her grandfather said, almost sadly. 'Your brother and sister have no hankering to leave home?'

'None at all. Paul loves it all so much, and I expect Nancy will marry one of the local boys and settle down. She's very pretty.'

'Well, if you don't hear soon, we'll do something about it,' Dr Baxter decided. 'I can't have you moping. You'll be giving my patients the wrong medicine, and getting me a bad name.'

He was unprepared for the way her face whitened.

'Oh, Grandfather, don't say that, even as a joke,' she whispered. 'You see, something like that almost happened to me once upon a time, and — and I lost my nerve . . . ' She began to tell him about it, and he listened, his eyes never leaving her face.

'But that was because you were so overworked,' he said. 'At least you're over it now.'

'Yes,' she agreed, 'I'm over it now. I had Ian to thank, largely, for that. I'll see you later, and if we're going to have a guest this evening, change that shirt.'

'It's clean!'

'I know, but it's also frayed at the collar. We don't want Dr Ferguson to be wondering how he can pay for his dinner tonight!'

She was grinning impishly, and he sat back, relieved. That was a bit more like his own Shirley!

Dr Peter Ferguson was an older man, with greying hair, and after she had helped him with a few problems, she asked him to come to supper that evening.

'It will only be plain food,' she said.

'Mrs Ross doesn't go in for anything fancy.'

'It will be a delight to me,' said Dr Ferguson. 'Since my wife died, I've been looking after myself. Coming up here to help Ian out is quite a break for me. Susan had a long illness.'

'Oh, I am sorry,' Shirley said sympathetically.

'She was a happy person,' he said. 'I miss her very much, but I hope I'll be able to find myself again, tramping among the hills.'

'You belong to Edinburgh?'

'Born and bred.'

Supper that evening was a happy meal, and Shirley was delighted to see that her grandfather and Dr Ferguson were getting on like a house on fire. They'd each had many years of practical experience, but in entirely different environments, and they found a fascination in comparing notes.

After a while, Shirley took little part in the conversation, her thoughts again with Neil. How would he fare in

Edinburgh? At least he would have pretty Joan Gibson to show him around.

*　*　*

The following evening, Shirley learned that Neil would probably have other company besides Joan, when Brigadier Maxwell called round for a return game of chess with Dr Baxter. This time the doctor was determined to win.

'I'm on my own again,' the Brigadier told them as he took off his coat. 'Catriona has decided she's going back to Edinburgh. She has had the chance of going to work in a beauty salon there, just as she did before. Oh, I don't blame her,' he added, sighing. 'There's nothing much for a girl here — yourself, excepted, of course, Dr Shirley,' he added hastily.

There would be nothing much for Catriona now that Neil had gone to Edinburgh, Shirley thought shrewdly.

'What are you doing then?' she

262

asked. 'I mean, how are you coping?'

'Oh, very well. Martha Paterson, who lives next door to old man Elliott, is cleaning up for me, and I can make a good curry, if I say so myself.'

Shirley grinned and went off to cut some sandwiches. Somehow her world seemed to be changing under her very nose. Neil had gone, and now Catriona, and Ian Andrews was now married and on his honeymoon.

Her thoughts went to Dr Ferguson. What if her grandfather decided to share the practice? He and Peter Ferguson seemed to get on very well indeed, and perhaps that sad-eyed man would enjoy living in Inverdorran for a while. He could soon find the peace and tranquillity he was looking for here, as she had herself. He might just be persuaded to stay on here if she landed that job in London.

Next morning, Shirley awoke to high winds and lashing rain against her window, and spent some time looking out her heavy boots and mackintosh.

The boots were too heavy to drive in, so she would have to zip them on every time she left the car.

'There's a letter for you from young Brian,' her grandfather said, and Shirley took it with a word of thanks. It was always pleasant hearing from Brian, and this one contained especially good news. He and Leila Reynolds were engaged!

If you manage to come down in, say, another week, he wrote, *then we'll hold an engagement party. Leila is adding a bit at the end of the letter.*

Leila's 'bit' seemed to ring with happiness, and Shirley's heart was warm for both of them.

'Grandfather, Brian is engaged! Isn't that wonderful? I'm going to London to the party. You'll manage, won't you?'

'Of course! I'm not in my dotage, you know. Tell Brian how happy I am for him,' he added dubiously. Well, bang went his hopes for Shirley and young Dr Wills!

'If you need help, perhaps we could

ask Dr Ferguson.'

'He's got his own work to do. I'm fine as I am,' he told her.

She sighed, thinking there wasn't much she could do with him when he was in an independent mood!

The telephone rang and she went to answer it, coming back a moment later.

'That's Mr Bruce from further up the glen. His wife is expecting another baby, and he says she doesn't seem so well. I didn't like her blood pressure last time I saw her.'

A gust of wind blew the rain against the window once more, and she shivered.

'If you're going out, Grandfather, mind you wrap up well, though I don't think there's very much to see to. I'll see Mrs Clark when I get back — it's those varicose veins — and I'll also call in on old Mr Dewar. I'll have to persuade him to have those ears of his syringed. I think he likes being deaf!'

'Well, mind how you go, my dear,' he told her, 'and don't drive with those boots on. You can't gauge your accelerator in footwear like that.'

She grinned, nodded and waved to him cheerfully.

The telephone shrilled again, and this time Mrs Ross called out that she would see to it.

'I'll take down the message, Doctor,' she said. 'It's maybe for Miss Shirley.'

Dr Baxter could hear her exclaiming, and repeating the message, but he was not paying too much attention. He looked out at the lashing rain. Normally he could take things in his stride, but weather like this made him feel his age.

Mrs Ross came rushing through like a blast out of a cannon.

'Oh, Doctor, it's a telegram . . . for Miss Shirley,' she said.

* * *

'Well, go on then, read it!' Dr Baxter said firmly to the trembling Mrs Ross.

'It's from her parents — *All four arriving in London 5 a.m. — staying* seven days in Old Abbey Hotel, then coming to Inverdorran. Getting in touch. Mother and Father. That's it.' Mrs Ross took a deep breath and looked at her employer.

Hamish Baxter felt his knees go weak.

'Och, if only Shirley had waited five minutes before she went out!' he exclaimed.

He went to look out of the window at the lowering sky, torrential rain and scudding clouds.

'This is an awful day for her to be out,' he said worriedly.

The hours seemed to drag past. Dr Baxter moved his chair to the window and took up his seat there, with a medical journal to read, though his eyes were oftener on the rain-swept road than on the book. The only figure he could see was young Jamie Fraser, David's son, clad in a navy-blue duffel coat.

Dr Baxter watched him struggling against the wind, then saw that young

Jamie was making for Beech House. Laying aside his journal, he hurried downstairs to let him in.

'This is no day for you to be out, Jamie,' he greeted him. 'Is there anything wrong, lad?'

'Mrs Watt at the post office sent me,' Jamie said, panting, his cheeks red as apples. 'They've been trying to get you on the phone, Doctor, but it looks as though the lines are down.'

'Yes. Out with it, lad.'

'The man said there's been an accident up the valley. The river is in spate and the Dorran Bridge has collapsed and — and a doctor is needed . . . '

Dr Baxter felt the blood drain from his face. Shirley would have had to cross the Dorran Bridge to reach the Grahams' home.

'What else did they say, Jamie?' he asked. 'Who's had the accident?'

'That was all, Doctor,' Jamie assured him earnestly, obviously relieved to have delivered his message. 'Can — can

I go home now?'

'Ay — wait a minute, Jamie.' The old man fished in his pocket and found a fifty pence piece.

'If you wait, I'll take you home in my car,' Dr Baxter offered, since it would not delay him. He would have to go straightaway.

'No, I can manage, Doctor,' Jamie said, and he thought how much the boy resembled his uncle, Neil Fraser.

It was a nightmare journey up the valley with the rain and wind lashing against the car. Here and there the winding road was flooded, but the car was a sturdy one, and Dr Baxter drove on doggedly. He was feeling a little tired now, with the excitement of Colin's telegram, and now this great fear in his heart as to what lay ahead at the Dorran Bridge.

As he neared the turn-off, he could see a few people gathered with storm lanterns, and there seemed to be one or two men manoeuvring with a tractor.

'What's wrong?' he asked, hurrying

out of the car. 'Where's the accident?'

'It's young Peter Harper,' one of the men told him, coming forward. 'He was on the bridge with his tractor when it collapsed, though luckily he was nearly over at this side. The tractor went in the river, but Peter was thrown on to the bank. He's unconscious, Doctor.'

'Is he the only casualty?' Dr Baxter asked sharply.

'Yes, Doctor, there was no-one else here.'

For the next half-hour, Dr Baxter forgot everything but the job on hand. Finally he was satisfied that his patient could be moved, and two of the men concerned in Mountain Rescue brought a stretcher and helped to take the young man home to his farm nearby.

Dr Baxter watched over him anxiously till his mother had him safely in bed, then gave him an injection.

'He'll come round fairly soon, and we'll see if he needs an ambulance, Mrs Harper, but it might not be necessary. Isn't it Peter who does a bit of boxing?'

'Yes, Doctor.'

'Then he's a fit boy. Don't worry about him. Er . . . ' He paused. 'Has there been any news from the other side of the river? My granddaughter is over there with young Mrs Graham.'

'Oh, she's had a baby girl,' said Mrs Harper. 'Dr Shirley managed to telephone before the wires came down. Imagine she'll be stuck at the Grahams' till the storm dies down. It's better now, I think. The rain doesn't seem to be so heavy.'

⋆   ⋆   ⋆

At home, Mrs Ross kept an anxious eye on the weather, not too happy about both Dr Baxter and Shirley being out, though it was not the first time she'd had to wait for the doctor when he was out on a case.

The telephone kept making ringing noises, then rang shrilly. It was the engineer to say it was fixed, and Mrs Ross lost no time in phoning Mrs Watt at the post office, who told her about Peter Harper and Mrs Graham.

Thankfully, Mrs Ross put down the telephone, and prepared to wait, but a moment later it shrilled again. This time it was a long-distance call, and she could hardly hear for crackling noises on the line.

'Hello, Mrs Ross? This is Neil Fraser.'

'Who? I can hardly hear . . . '

'Neil Fraser.'

'Oh — it's yourself then, Mr Fraser . . . '

'Yes. I've just seen the TV news,' Neil shouted, 'about the Dorran Bridge being down — and the accident, and a doctor being called . . . '

'Oh — on the news, did you say, Mr Fraser?'

'Yes. Is — is Dr Shirley OK?'

'She's up the valley at the Grahams'. Dr Baxter saw to young Peter Harper at Dorran Bridge.'

Neil's voice faded and then the line crackled again and Mrs Ross gave up the attempt to understand.

'I'll tell Dr Shirley you called, Mr Fraser,' she shouted, and hung up the telephone.

The storm subsided in another hour, and shortly afterwards, Dr Baxter got home again, and was glad to go to his bed.

'Dr Ferguson has been here,' Mrs Ross told him. 'He says he'll look after any calls for you, and Mr Fraser called, too.'

'Thanks, Mrs Ross,' he said gratefully. 'I won't deny I need my bed.'

★   ★   ★

Shirley came home the following day, a makeshift bridge having been thrown over the river, and everything else was forgotten in the excitement of learning that her family were in London.

'You go and see them, Shirley,' her grandfather said. 'Let them know how welcome they'll be in Inverdorran.'

She looked at his slightly anxious eyes. The waiting time must be a bit of strain for him until he met her father again. Maybe she could pave the way.

'You can't be left on your own to see to the practice,' she said. 'Unless — I wonder if Dr Ferguson would help? Ian and Alison are due back this week from their honeymoon.'

'I'll get him on the phone now,' said the old man, and hurried away.

On Friday, Shirley made the long journey to London by train, then by taxi to the hotel where her parents were staying. It seemed to her that with every yard she travelled, her heart beat faster and faster. Her mind was swirling round. Would Paul and Nancy have changed? Was Dad fully recovered?

She had booked a room and knew that they were expecting her, but the thrill of seeing her own people again was almost too much, as she hugged her mother and father, then turned to Paul and Nancy. They had seemed like children to her when she left New Zealand, but now they were quite grown up.

'My Place Is With You'

'It will be very hard for your father to leave Grandfather Baxter here when we all go home,' Kate Baxter said thoughtfully. 'He's an old man now. We're thinking he might like to come with us, Shirley.'

'Oh, he won't want to leave Inverdorran, Mum,' Shirley said quickly.

'We were hoping you'd put it to him, dear,' said her mother. 'At his age, it's his own people who count, not where he lives, and he'll want to be with your father, and you, too. You seem to have grown very attached to one another.'

'Yes,' Shirley agreed, though her eyes were troubled. She felt she could not persuade her grandfather to live in New Zealand, and hoped she would be able to make her mother understand.

'Would — would you really want that for us, Mum?' she asked. 'I mean . . . '

Kate Baxter looked squarely at her daughter. Shirley had not confided in her, but she could see that her elder daughter was not really happy here. She was not the same girl she had been.

'Yes,' she said firmly, 'that's what I want. I think we should all go back home, Shirley.'

Nancy came hurrying into the dining-room, where Shirley and her mother were helping to set the table.

'There's a young man to see you, Shirley,' she said. 'He's waiting in the lounge. He's sure dishy, Shirl.'

Her sister grinned. Nancy was at the age when she was very interested in the appearance of most young men. It was no doubt a patient who wanted something.

She removed her pretty frilly apron and handed it to Nancy.

'You whip the cream for Mrs Ross, then,' she said, and walked through to the lounge.

Then her heart gave a great lurch as she turned after shutting the door, and saw Neil rising to his feet and turning to greet her.

For a long moment, Shirley stared at Neil, her heart beating loudly enough for her to hear, then she could see that the delight on his face reflected her own.

'Neil!' The next moment she was in his powerful arms and he was kissing her tenderly. He was no longer the tired, uncertain invalid, but once again strong and determined as she had known him when she first came to Inverdorran.

'You're so much better,' she said, her eyes shining, when she got her breath back.

'Completely better, darling,' he said. 'I feel as though I've come home from a long journey, to find you waiting. But I seem to have wasted such a lot of time, Shirley, and want to get on with my life. Will you marry me? You must know I've been in love with you from the beginning.'

'From the beginning?' she teased.

'Yes, a brisk young doctor in a hired car drove up to Inverdorran and straight into my heart. I was never free of you after that, and I won't be really fit and well till you've said yes.'

'That's blackmail.'

'It is.'

'Then I'll have to accept,' she said, as they laughed joyfully together.

'The complex is being opened on Saturday,' he told her. 'I did most of the arranging by phone from Edinburgh, and Alec Meldrum has agreed to open it.'

'Yes, I heard that a famous swimmer could be in our midst.'

'It's very good of him to spare the time, but, of course, he's very interested. David has had to do most of the work recently, but I'll be able to take over from now on. Edinburgh seemed to put new life into me, and Joan looked after me so well. She even gave up some of her free time when she could have been out with Martin.'

'Martin?'

'Martin Jameson, her fiancé. He used to come and play chess with me. The Gibsons were really wonderful, all of them, and I can never be too grateful. I hope to take you to meet them some time.'

Shirley nodded. She felt, suddenly, that she'd played only a small part in his recovery, and Neil pulled her into his arms again, able to read her expressive face.

'Surely you must realise I only wanted to be near you as a whole person,' he said gently. 'I hated you to see me ill.'

She nodded, understanding. 'Yes, I can see that.' She hesitated for a moment, feeling that there was one more point to clear up. 'What about Catriona Maxwell? Did you see her at all?'

'Yes, she came to see me, and I called in at her salon before I left Edinburgh, to invite her to our Grand Opening on Saturday. I doubt if she'll be there, though. Oh, you've no need to worry about Catriona, darling. She's truly happy at last.

'The salon is everything she dreamed it could be and it means everything to her. Catriona will work all day, and every day, and no doubt her salon will become famous all over Edinburgh, and beyond. She's got what she really wanted.'

'I'm so glad about that,' Shirley said, but as she looked up into Neil's dark face, radiant with excitement, she wondered a little but kept her thoughts to herself.

Deep inside she knew that as well as loving him, they were right for one another and she was deeply content. Catriona could never have loved him as she did.

'I believe your parents are here from New Zealand,' he said.

'That's right. In fact, we'll go through and I'll introduce you to . . . ' She broke off, suddenly remembering her mother had set her heart on them all going back to New Zealand, but there could be no question of that if she married Neil. This news would have to be broken to her a bit more gently.

★　★　★

Seeing her hesitation, and the doubt on her face, the eager light died a little from Neil's eyes.

'I — I'd better go now then, Shirley,' he began, but she quickly caught his hand.

'No, don't misunderstand, darling. It's just that Mother is hoping I'll go back to New Zealand with the family and — and coax Grandfather to go as well. She feels that the whole family would settle down better back home.'

'I see,' he said, and also saw that there could only be honesty between them. 'Shirley, darling, you must surely see how much I love you, and how much you mean to me, but the sports complex is going to mean a lot to a great many people, and I . . . '

'Say no more, Neil,' she said gently.

'I've promised to marry you, and my place is here, with you, in Inverdorran. I'll tell my parents tonight about our new plans. I think it's better that I should do it myself.'

'Very well, but I'll call back here tomorrow, if I may. I think I ought to have a word with your parents, don't you?'

'Of course,' Shirley agreed. 'We'll expect you to dinner tomorrow evening.'

'I'll be here,' he promised, and quietly she closed the front door after him, and went to join the family in the dining-room.

As soon as she walked into the dining-room, Shirley felt something was amiss, as five pairs of eyes turned to regard her silently.

'I've just been telling Grandfather that he would be most welcome to make his home with us in New Zealand,' Kate Baxter said, smiling at Shirley. 'You tell him how much he'd love it, Shirley, and how much we would love to have him there. There's always a crying need for doctors, too, and there's no reason why you can't both work together, over there, just as you do here.'

Grandfather Baxter gazed at Shirley broodingly, and she could see the doubt in his eyes, and the deep loneliness at the prospect of being on his own again. Yet she knew how much he loved Inverdorran, and his dream had been that his family would settle here again, one day.

Now he knew Colin had made his real home in New Zealand, and would never come home, and the old man was obviously trying to face facts.

'So you're going back to New Zealand, Shirley,' he said heavily.

Shirley sat down, and looked at her mother, but the joy and happiness she felt by accepting Neil's proposal could no longer be hidden.

'I — I'm sorry, Mum,' she said, 'and Dad . . . I'm really sorry, but I can't. I want to stay here in Inverdorran. That was Neil Fraser, Grandfather, and he's better now. He — he asked me to marry him and I've said yes.'

Colin Baxter saw the delight on his father's face with a momentary pang. There had been peace and contentment in his heart as he had walked with his father once more, and he had hoped they would never be parted again. But here was the answer for all to see.

Dr Baxter wanted to stay at home.

But it was to her mother that Shirley now turned. Paul and Nancy were full of excitement, now that they knew their sister was going to marry the man who was the driving force behind the sports complex, but Mrs Baxter knew that this next parting with Shirley would be the one which mattered.

She had missed her elder daughter when she first came to the London hospital, but it had seemed a temporary parting. Now Shirley would be staying in Scotland for ever.

'Oh, Shirley,' she whispered.

'Just wait till you meet Neil, Mum,'

Shirley told her. 'You'll be glad for me then.'

Mrs Baxter spent the following day making a special celebration dinner for that evening, ably assisted by Mrs Ross, who was happy to keep in the background this time.

That evening, dressed in a long apricot velvet skirt and cream blouse, Shirley was waiting for Neil, and was very proud of him as she took him into the lounge to meet her family.

Mrs Baxter looked from the tall, dark young man to the radiant face of her daughter, and was content. Shirley had got what she wanted.

She could see honesty and integrity in the young man, as he shook hands with her and Colin, then with Paul and Nancy who were inclined to regard him as a hero.

But it was Dr Baxter whose joy

seemed as great as that of Neil and Shirley.

'I'm proud to have you as a grandson, Neil,' he said. 'I couldn't have done better if I'd made the choice myself.'

* * *

On Saturday evening, Shirley could feel the air of excitement sweeping all over Inverdorran. The new sports complex had been designed by a genius, and seemed to fit into the place as though Inverdorran had been built for it, instead of the other way round.

It was adequate in every way, without being overpowering, and the architect had wisely allowed the natural beauty of its surroundings to be the best form of landscape.

Dr Ferguson had stayed on, and he and Ian had promised to take any special calls for Dr Baxter and Shirley.

'Nobody seems to want to be ill today!' Ian laughed. 'In fact, all my patients are insisting there's nothing wrong with them, and are crawling out of bed! I've been coaxing old Hannah Price to get on her feet for weeks, but it takes this new sports complex to winkle her out.'

'When she sees Alec Meldrum she might even take up swimming!' Shirley joked, and Ian's eyes sobered.

'That might not be such a bad idea,' he said. 'Oh, I don't mean for Hannah, of course, but the sports complex is going to be excellent therapy for some people.'

Somehow events seemed to be whirling her along, Shirley thought, as she hurried from one job to the next. The day before, she and Neil had driven up to Inverness to visit a jeweller's, where she chose a lovely ring of three matching diamonds.

'One for each of us, and one for our future,' said Neil. 'I feel that it is diamond bright.'

'I'll remind you of that one day!' Shirley told him, though the ring sparkling on her finger gave her deep inward happiness.

The date for their wedding was set for next month, so Shirley and her mother found each day was short as they sent out invitations, and made arrangements for the thousand-and-one things that had to be seen to.

Nancy, who was to be Shirley's only bridesmaid, made a sudden decision to start dieting and lose two inches off her waist.

'I'm glad for you, Shirley. Truly, darling,' Mrs Baxter told her.

'I know,' said Shirley. 'Thanks, Mum. I'm so glad you, Dad and the kids are going to stay to see me through the wedding — it just wouldn't be the same without you.'

'I know, love. You didn't really think that we could all go home and miss the happiest day of your life, did you?'

There were tears glistening in Shirley's eyes as her mother spoke. Then, suddenly, mother and daughter were in each other's arms, laughing and crying at the same time.

On Saturday the main stadium of the sports complex was packed to capacity with everyone agog to see Alec Meldrum, the fine swimmer whose face was so familiar on television, and above newspaper articles. He had arrived from Inverness, and Neil and David Fraser had spent some time showing him all over the complex.

Later, Shirley joined them for lunch, though she allowed the three men to do most of the talking.

This was Neil's big day, and David's. She felt very proud and humble to be part of it.

★   ★   ★

Sitting on a platform rigged up in the main stadium, banked with flowers, Shirley had time to look round at the people who had gathered to launch the new venture.

She could see Brigadier Maxwell, as tall and well groomed as ever, his hair a silver halo round his head. Catriona was sitting beside him, looking breathtakingly lovely.

Over to the right, she could see Mr and Mrs Sinclair with Geoffrey Lewis beside them. As usual, Geoffrey was talking sixty to the dozen, and Shirley was amused to see that he had his tape recorder at the ready.

He must surely be the newest convert to Neil's scheme, she thought, and he certainly never did things by halves. Most of Inverdorran must know by now that Geoffrey now heartily approved of the sports complex, and was planning to take up hurdling.

With his long thin legs, he could easily be good at it, Shirley thought, with a smile.

Neil had now introduced Alec Meldrum, who got up to make an excellent speech about sport in Britain and to give encouragement to a great many young people who might want to take up any particular sport for recreation.

Paul and Nancy were listening, open

mouthed, as were many young people in the audience.

Then Shirley heard her own name mentioned, and suddenly there was thunderous applause all round her as Neil took her hand, and pulled her to her feet.

Alex Meldrum had announced their very new engagement!

Blushing, Shirley felt tears pricking behind her eyelids as she sensed the waves of good wishes washing towards her and Neil from every corner. Smiling, she could see all their friends looking towards both of them, and wishing them every happiness.

Later, as Shirley and Neil walked back towards Beech House, Inverdorran seemed to be back to normal again, though with a subtle difference. Where once it had seemed rather sleepy, now it was vibrant with life and promise for the future.

The late afternoon sun lit up the hedgerows, and as they walked along, side by side, Neil took Shirley's hand.

'Happy, darling?' he asked.

Shirley nodded, her eyes on Beech House, as they rounded the corner. Whatever lay ahead in the future for her and Neil, Dr Baxter's granddaughter felt she had come home.

THE END

DANGER COMES CALLING

Karen Abbott

Elaine Driscoe and her sister Kate expect their walking holiday along Offa's Dyke Path to be a peaceful pursuit — until a chance encounter with a mysterious stranger casts a shadow of fear over everything. Their steps are constantly crossed by three men — Niall, Steve and Phil. But which of them can they trust? And what is the ultimate danger that awaits them in Prestatyn?

NO SUBSTITUTE FOR LOVE

Dina McCall

Although recently made redundant, nurse Holly Fraser decides to spend some of her savings on a Christmas coach tour in Scotland. When the tour reaches the Callender Hotel, several people mistake Holly for a Mrs MacEwan. Furthermore, Ian MacEwan arrives to take her to the Hall, convinced that she is his wife, Carol! Although Ian despises Carol for having deserted him and their two small children, two-year-old Lucy needs her mother. Holly stays to help the child, but finds herself in an impossible situation.

LOVE'S SWEET SECRETS

Bridget Thorn

When her parents die, Melanie comes home to run their guest house and to try to win the Jubilee Prize for her father's garden. But her sister, Angela, wants her to sell the property, and her boyfriend, Michael, wants a partnership and marriage. Just before the Spring opening, Paul Hunt arrives and helps Melanie when the garden is attacked by vandals. After the news is splashed over the national papers, guests cancel. Then real danger threatens. But who is the enemy?

OUT OF THE SHADOWS

Judy Chard

Why does Carol Marsh, the new receptionist at the country inn in Devon, have to report to the police regularly? Why does she never ask for time off and rejects all attempts by the owner, Norman Willis, to be friendly? Then, Norman's wife is found dead in suspicious circumstances. Could Carol have had some part in her death? Yvonne's relationship with her husband had deteriorated since Carol's arrival. Maybe Carol and Norman have a deeper, more sinister relationship than that of employer and employee.

THE MIRACLE OF LOVE

June Gadsby

When Holly's much longed-for promotion goes to handsome outsider Joel Richards, she has reason to suspect that something mysterious is going on. This is confirmed when Joel replaces the store's regular Santa Claus with yet another outsider and there follows a string of Christmas burglaries. With her career in jeopardy and the interests of her young clients at heart, Holly decides to investigate and ends up being more involved with her new boss than she ever imagined possible.